Edward Frederic Benson was born at Wellington College, Berkshire, in 1867. He was one of an extraordinary family. His father Edward White Benson – first headmaster of Wellington – later became Chancellor of Lincoln Cathedral, Bishop of Truro, and Archbishop of Canterbury. His mother, Mary Sidgwick, was described by Gladstone as 'the cleverest woman in Europe'. Two children died young but the other four, bachelors all, achieved distinction: Arthur Christopher as Master of Magdalene College, Cambridge, and a prolific author; Maggie as an amateur egyptologist; Robert Hugh as a Catholic priest and propagandist novelist; and Fred.

Like his brothers and sisters, Fred was a precocious scribbler. He was still a student at Cambridge when he published his first book, *Sketches from Marlborough*. While he was working as an archaeologist in Athens, his first novel *Dodo* (1893) was published to great success. Thereafter Benson devoted himself to writing, playing sports, watching birds, and gadding about. He mixed with the best and brightest of his day: Margot Asquith, Marie Corelli, his mother's friend Ethel Smyth and many other notables found their eccentricities exposed in the shrewd, hilarious world of his fiction.

Around 1918, E. F. Benson moved to Rye, Sussex. He was inaugurated mayor of the town in 1934. There in his garden room, the collie Taffy beside him, Benson wrote many of his comical novels, his sentimental fiction, ghost stories, informal biographies and reminiscences – almost one hundred books in all. Ten days before his death on 29 February 1940, E. F. Benson delivered to his publisher a last autobiography, *Final Edition*.

The Hogarth Press also publishes *Mrs Ames, Paying Guests, Secret Lives, As We Are, As We Were, Dodo – An Omnibus* and *The Luck of the Vails*.

The Comedy Scene.

THE
FREAKS OF
MAYFAIR

E. F. Benson

Illustrations by George Plank

New Introduction by
Christopher Hawtree

THE HOGARTH PRESS
LONDON

DEDICATED TO
FRANK EYES
AND
KINDLY EARS

Published in 1986 by
The Hogarth Press
Chatto & Windus Ltd
40 William IV Street, London WC2N 4DF

First published in Great Britain by T. N. Foulis 1916
Hogarth edition offset from original British edition
Copyright the Executors of the Estate of the Reverend K. S. P. McDowall
Introduction copyright © Christopher Hawtree 1986

British Library Cataloguing in Publication Data

Benson, E.F.
The freaks of Mayfair
I. Title
823'.8[F]   PR6003.E66
ISBN   0 7012 0697 7

Printed in Great Britain by
Cox & Wyman Ltd
Reading, Berkshire

INTRODUCTION

At the end of 1916, six months after the beginning of the Somme offensive, an anonymous reviewer in *The Times Literary Supplement* was reading the latest E. F. Benson. The worldly characters depicted in this collection of society sketches, apparently untouched by the horrors of France, he feared, were 'too invertebrate to turn and say: "How came you, brother, when paper is so dear, to describe us in a rivulet of print meandering thro' a meadow of margin?" '

Evidently the reviewer did not remember *Mike*, a novel which Benson had published in the middle of that year (shortly after another, *David Blaize*). Here, English and German characters are indeed made aware of the war, an agony which the reader shares, but only as a reaction to the painful sentimentality on display. Over the next eighteen months Benson made amends for this by compiling reports about the history and present condition of Turkey and Poland. Lucid as these are, it is in the transitory nature of political upheaval that they should not continue to engage much interest.

Appearing as it did, when faces were being trodden deeper in the mud by the next contingent to go over the top, one should not be altogether surprised that *The Freaks of Mayfair*, too, has become neglected. Little noticed at the time, it was duly submerged by the flow of writing which Benson maintained for another twenty-five years. Only now can the book's significance be appreciated, for it marks a distinct turning-point in Benson's career, one which heralds a magnificent late period of startling unexpectedness.

Benson is not widely regarded as possessing a 'tragic vision', but the war brought out that real humour which is its near ally, and which had been subsumed in his Edwardian novels (two or more of which appeared every year) by light comedy of a sort that now makes for heavy going. Rather than heightening his characters' absurdities, Benson's humour had merely indulged them. In *The Oakleyites* (1915), however, there is a novelist, Wilfred Easton, who presents a telling *apologia*. He says to his mother:

You find all that I write so absolutely unreadable. I used to watch you with pain attempting to get through any book of mine; but now I watch you with amusement when I see you skipping wildly when you think I am not observing you, and falling asleep when you try to be conscientious . . . I don't write as the birds sing, because I must, but because I like doing it, and because I thereby gain a very comfortable livelihood. There really is no necessity for an ironmonger's mother to be enamoured of garden-hoes. But people with gardens happen to want them, and he supplies them at a decent profit. In the same way people in villas like to know about Marchionesses, so I tell them about people whom I call Marchionesses. It doesn't hurt the Marchionesses. But you see the ordinary middle-class public want to know what happens in Mayfair. That is why I lay my scenes there.

This is not a cynical discourse, such as might gain an approving nod from the author of *Lace* and *Lace 2*, for he continues:

Now don't be *banal*, and tell me that to write pot-boilers spoils your talent, if you happen to have any. It does nothing of the kind. It merely keeps your pen in practice for the happy day, should it ever arrive, when you have something authentic, something of your own to say.

Benson himself had already written two 'shockers', *The Luck of the Vails* and *The Blotting Book*, which, rigorously told, rise above the cloying prose of the novels that surround them, but his reputation rested on the pot-boilers which were popular enough in the villas to inspire three publishers to issue collections of saws and apophthegms from them.

On the surface, this book of sketches might have appeared orthodox enough. It resembles many of those fostered by the buoyant magazine market, which had already inspired Benson's genial *Book of Months* and *The Babe B.A.* – an impression perhaps confirmed for them by its being published as a companion volume to Ian Hay's jejune, highly popular *The Lighter Side of School Life*. Readers familiar with these and with Benson's sentimental comedies might not have grasped the full import of a title, *The Freaks of Mayfair*, which likens the inhabitants of Curzon Street to those of a side-show in an American travelling circus.

A human vanity too blinkered to be aware of its own futility sustains this series of variations: taken together, these sketches present a world of grotesque and horrifying decay, one that is made all the worse for its pretence of good breeding and taste. 'The pity of it all is the appalling waste among asps of brains, inventive faculty, and humour,' concludes our guide to one branch of the species. 'If only their gifts were used to some laudable or even innocent purpose, the world in general would gain a great deal of entertainment, and the asps of the popularity and success that they secretly crave for. As it is, some part of moral ptomaine has infected them, some invasion of microbes that turns their wit into poison.'

Although the war sharpened and darkened Benson's humour (a process compounded by the deaths of his mother, a sister, Maggie, and brother, Hugh), he did not become merely sour and descend to invective, for he realised that this soon becomes as stale as old light comedy. This book of despatches from the home front is finely balanced: a detail or two, elegantly related, is suffcient to convict, and dignified enough to avoid charges of persecution. In the years to come, 'Aunt Georgie' would leave these pages and join other characters, Lucia and Miss Mapp among them, who speak up for themselves while the narrator's discretion does not diminish a fine sense of ridicule.

Such a spirit is matched here by George Plank's illustrations. For all the echoes of Beardsley, it is Benson's characters that one sees: their myriad rolling chins, sagging cheeks, beringed fingers, darting eyes; and the ageing man who 'brushes his hair very carefully now, not knowing that to the disinterested observer the top of his head looks rather like music paper, with white gaps in between the lines, and that it is quite obvious that he grows those thinning locks very long on one side of his head (just above the ear) and trains them in the manner of an espaliered pear over the denuded bone where once a plume used jauntily to erect itself' – if the ad men have got their marketing right, such troubled characters ply the escalators every day.

Plank had arrived from Philadelphia in May 1914 in the company of a *littérateur*, James Whitall, and his wife, who had decided that 'the kind of life we wanted could be more easily lived in England than in America'. Whitall duly turned down the chance of translating Proust and of working at The Hogarth Press, settling instead for a stint on Squire's *London Mercury* and reading for Heinemann. 'I am a little alarmed by the social values of Mr Whitall,' noted Virginia Woolf, 'for we don't want the Press to be a fashionable hobby patronised and inspired by Chelsea.'

Plank, meanwhile, soon prospered. As Whitall records in an unduly long memoir, *English Years*, within weeks of arriving, and war notwithstanding, they had discovered the fringes of Bloomsbury and Cheyne Row:

Plank's circle of friends increased to unmanageable proportions and it is to his everlasting credit that he did not allow his art to be submerged during the years he spent in the Thurloe Square studio. Those who made demands upon his time were often impossible to resist, but he managed in some miraculous way to accomplish his yearly quota of covers for *Vogue*, his various illustrations and book-plates engraved on wood [including Benson's] and his many black and white drawings. The delicacy of his line, his exquisite use of colour and the richness of his imagination were unsurpassed in his particular field.

He even survived the demands made upon him by Vita Sackville-West's obstreperous mother, with whom he kept up a gossipy correspondence, and he died, aged eighty-two, in 1965, a world away, as one might think, from that pictured in these pages.

Time has blurred London's geography, but the freaks remain. Sometimes they are evident from afar; sometimes they become apparent only after prolonged exposure. Benson can scarcely have conceived of a fume-ridden Chelsea upon whose pavements loll doped-up, tattooed and manacled youths with hair jauntily erected into multi-coloured shapes that resemble spikes rather than plumes. He would, however, have looked further, his eye picking out those less obviously freakish in appearance and behaviour but no less absurd for that. As Anthony Burgess puts it in an essay on Leslie Fiedler's study of the 'freak' phenomenon, 'the study of mankind is of a being absurd, pitiable, unstable, endlessly fascinating, and that is what we mean by a freak'.

The ridiculous increases in proportion to the seriousness with which it is regarded. At times it remains harmless, even if the adherents do not care to be reminded of it when fashion changes; at others, fostered by a sterner vanity, it can prove dangerous: how did a figure as absurd as Hitler come to dominate a country? What is certain is that few people care to turn upon themselves that merciless eye which is so pleasurable when E. F. Benson directs it at others. *Pace* the reviewer in *The Times Literary Supplement*, Benson himself realised that it is the lack of such clear vision that brings about war between nations or, of more immediate concern to his future readers, the decorous hostilities enjoyed by those redoubtable ladies in Tilling.

Christopher Hawtree, Newbold Heath 1986

THE LIST OF CONTENTS

THE LIST OF ILLUSTRATIONS

reproduced from drawings by
GEORGE PLANK

THE COMPLEAT SNOBS
CHAPTER ONE

CHAPTER ONE
THE COMPLEAT SNOBS

THERE IS NO MORE JOYOUS couple in all Mayfair than Sir Louis Marigold, Bart, M.P., and Lady Mary Marigold, and whether they are at Marigold Park, Bucks, or at Homburg, or in their spacious residence in Berkeley Square, their lives form one unbroken round of pomp and successful achievement. She was the daughter of an obscure Irish Earl, and when she married her husband was still hard at work building up the business of Marigold & Sons. Those were strenuous days, and the profession of money-getting made it necessary for him to indulge his snobbishness only as a hobby. But she, like the good wife she has always been to him, took care of his hobby, as of a stamp-collection, and constantly enriched it with specimens of her own acquisition, being a snob of purest ray serene herself. She is the undoubted descendant of Arrahmedear, king of Donegal, in which salubrious county her brother, the present Earl, is steadily drinking himself to death in the intervals of farming his fifty-acre estate. When he has succeeded in completely poisoning himself with whisky, she will become Countess of Ballamuck herself, since the title descends,

15

THE FREAKS OF MAYFAIR

in default of male heirs, in the female line, and
there will be what I hope it is not irreverent to
call high old times in Berkeley Square and Marigold Park.

When first they married her husband always
playfully called her 'The Princess' (being the
lineal descendant of that remarkable monarch
King Arrahmedear), and what began in play
soon sobered into a habit. But when she is a
real contemporary peeress, it is probable that he
will drop the appellation derived from legend-
ary kings, and call her Countess. There will be
no hint of badinage about that: Countess she
will be, and the papers will be full of little paragraphs about the movements of Sir Louis Marigold, Bart., M.P., and the Countess of Ballamuck. . . . There is just the faintest suggestion
of Ouida-ism and impropriety which gives such
announcements a peculiar relish.

Now there is no snob so profound as the
well-born snob, especially in the female line.
She (in this case Lady Mary Marigold) knows
about it from the inside, and is aware of all it
means to be the daughter of earls, not to mention kings. Her husband therefore, having been
born of an obscure commercial family, was not
originally so gifted as his wife, but by industry

16

and study he has now practically caught her up, and they run together in an amicable rose-coloured dead-heat. Like all the finer endowments, as that of poetry, pure snobbishness is born not acquired, and lowly as was his birth, the fairy-godmother who visited his infant cradle brought this golden gift with her, and with the same instinct for what is worth having that has always distinguished him, he did not squander or dissipate her bounty, but hoarded and polished and perfected it. When he was quite a little boy he used to dream about marquises, and, if a feverish cold added a touch of daring to his slumbers, about kings and queens; now with the reward that waits upon childhood's aspirations, it has all come true. Already his son (the first-born of the future countess) has married the Lady Something Something, daughter of a marquis, and there are great hopes about a widowed Bishop for his daughter.

It might seem that this episcopal anchorage was but a poor fulfilment of the prayers of her papa, but any who think that can form no adequate impression of the completeness of Sir Louis's snobbishness. For the real snob is he who worships success and distinction whether that success is hall-marked with coronets, wealth, or gaiters. To achieve success in the eyes of the world is to him the greatest of human accomplishments, and to be acquainted, or better still, connected with those who have done so, and best of all to be identified with them, constitutes the joy of life. Sir Louis has a profound admiration for his wife, his son, his son's wife, but he perhaps reserves his levels of highest complacency for himself, and with all his busy loving glances at the dazzling objects round him, he never really diverts his gaze from his own career. It is for his own success in life that he reserves his most sincere respect.

While his wife and he are thus in every sense perfect snobs, as far as perfection can be attained in this tentative world, they, like all other professors in great branches of knowledge, specialize in one particular department, and theirs is Birth. It is, of course, a great joy to Lady Mary Marigold to see the wife of a Cabinet Minister, of an African explorer, of an ambassador pass out of her dining-room at the conclusion of dinner, while she stands by the door and, shaking an admonitory finger at her husband till her bracelets rattle, says, ' Now, Sir Baronet, don't be too long'; it is a joy also to him to move to the other end of the table between the ambassador and

THE COMPLEAT SNOBS

the Cabinet Minister and say, ' My lady won't grudge your Excellency time to drink another glass of port and have a small cigar'; but most of all they love the hour when these manœuvres are enacted with members of the aristocracy, or, as has happened several times in this last year or two (for they are really among the tree-tops), with those for whom, to the exclusion of themselves and other guests, finger-bowls are provided. On these occasions, that is when Royalty is present, a sort of seizure is liable to come upon them, and for a minute or two one or other sinks back in his chair in a dazed condition consequent upon so much happiness. A foretaste of the bliss of Nirvana is theirs, and Sir Louis's eyes have been known to fill with happy, happy tears on seeing a Prince show my lady how to eat a cherry backwards, stalk first.

In the early days of their marriage, when, as Mr. Marigold, he came back tired with his day's work to his modest dwelling in Oakley Street, Birth was his hobby, and instead of relaxing his tired brain over the perusal of trashy novels or the playing of fruitless games of patience, like so many who have no sense of the value of time, he and she would sit tranquilly, one on each side of the fireplace, with a reading-lamp conveniently

19

placed between them, and dive into the sunlit waters of the Peerage. One happy Christmas Day they found that the present of each to the other was a copy of this beautiful book, and after this delicious coincidence, they kept the pleasant custom up, and always presented each other with Peerages at Christmas, so that now they have both of them a complete set for the last twenty-three years. Their son, Oswald Owen Vivian Lancelot, was true to parental tradition and tendency, and rapturous was the day when, at the age of fourteen, after hours of careful work, he gave his mother on her birthday the gift he had been secretly preparing for her, namely the roll of his own ancestry, neatly illuminated. It was somewhat lop-sided, for very few Marigolds had been discoverable, but away, away back went the other line of the descent through Earls and coronets innumerable till it reached the original and unique King Arrahmedear of Donegal, above whose glorious name he had illuminated a royal crown. It was entirely Oswald Owen Vivian Lancelot's own idea, and when he became engaged to the daughter of a marquis, his mother felt that she had known it would happen for years.

Owing probably to the large number of Jews

THE COMPLEAT SNOBS

and journalists and brewers and pawnbrokers
who have been ennobled during the long Liberal
tenure of office, this particular brand of snobbishness has rather fallen into neglect, and many of
the brightest snobs of Mayfair consider the cult
of the mere peerage a somewhat Victorian pursuit. But the more earnest practitioners, like
Lady Mary and Sir Louis Marigold, remain un-
affected by such shallowness. They argue that
the conferring of a peerage is still a symbol of
success, and, loyalist to the core, consider that
those who are good enough for the King are good
enough for them. Besides, they have found by
experience that they actually do feel greater raptures in the presence of Royalty than in that of
subjects of the realm, and among subjects of the
realm they like dukes better than marquises,
marquises than earls, earls than viscounts. It is
not implied that the pleasureableness of their
internal sensations would indicate to them the
rank of a total stranger whose name they were
ignorant of, but knowing his name and his rank,
they find that their delight in converse with him
increases according to his precedence. Many
pleasures are wholly matters of the imagination,
and this may be one, but the hallucination is in
this case, as in that of other nervous disorders,

21

THE FREAKS OF MAYFAIR

quite complete. And when a year or two ago
Lady Mary was dangerously ill with appendicitis, her husband sensibly assuaged the deep
and genuine anxiety he felt for her, by going
through, day after day, the cards of the eminent
people who had called to make enquiries. A
prince (a very eminent one) was so condescend-
ing as to call twice, once on a Monday and once
on the following Thursday. To this day Sir
Louis cannot but believe that the better news the
doctor gave him about my lady on that happy
afternoon, was somehow connected with the
magic of this repeated visit.

It has been mentioned that Sir Louis is in
the habit of calling his wife ' Princess '; it has
also been hinted that she alludes to him as 'Sir
Baronet.' There is a touch of badinage, of play-
fulness in both these titles, but below the play-
fulness is a substratum of seriousness. For she
is descended from kings so ancient that nobody
knows anything about them, and he is a real
Baronet, and since his title in ordinary use is
that of a mere knight, she and others of their in-
timates are accustomed to call him Sir Baronet,
in order to mark the difference between him and
such people as provincial mayors or eminent
actors and musicians. It must be supposed, too,

that he is far from discouraging this, since he has printed on his cards, 'Sir Louis Marigold, Bart., M. P.,' in full. It may be unusual, but then there are, unfortunately, not many Baronets who take a proper pride in the honours with which their Sovereign has decorated them or their ancestors. Marquises and earls put the degree of their nobility on their cards instead of just calling themselves 'Lord,' and surely a Baronet cannot go wrong in following so august an example. But there is another custom of his to which perhaps exception may be taken, for it is his habit when entertaining a luncheon-party at which mere commoners are present (this is not a frequent occurrence) to step jauntily along in his proper precedence to the dining-room, leaving the less exalted persons to follow. He does it in a careless, unconscious manner, and this manner is by no means put on: he walks in front of lowlier commoners instinctively: he does not think about it: his legs just take him. It is perhaps scarcely necessary to add that instinct is not so strong with him as to go in before any lady, even if she were his own washerwoman, for the obligations of chivalry outweigh with him even those of nobility. It has always been so with the true aristocrat, and it is so with him. Perhaps if a

23

THE FREAKS OF MAYFAIR

Suffragette were present he might go on ahead, for he considers that all women who hold any views but his on that subject have unsexed themselves. In his more indulgent moments he alludes to them as 'deluded wretches.'

His politics are of course Tory. A Tory Prime Minister honoured himself by recommending the King to honour Sir Louis, and much time and a good deal of money spent in the Tory cause make it quite likely that a further honour will some time be conferred upon him when (and if) his party ever gets back into power. It is significant, anyhow, that he has made several visits lately to the Heralds' College, where the shape of Viscounts' coronets seemed to interest him a good deal, for since the motto of his business life, which has proved so successful, was ' Prepare well in advance,' it is likely that it will apply in such matters as these as well, and it may safely be assumed that on that happy day his spoons and forks will be found to be already engraved with the honour conferred on him. To be sure, should this happen before Lady Mary's brother finally succumbs to the insidious bottle, she will find herself a step lower than her previous rank had been, by becoming a Viscountess instead of remaining an Earl's daughter. But, on the other hand, this will be but a temporary eclipse, for it cannot be so very long before she comes from under her cloud again on the demise of the dipsomaniac, and shines forth as an independent Countess. The whole affair, moreover, has been talked out so constantly by them that they are sure to have come to a wise decision based on the true principles of snobbishness.

Snobbishness is no superficial thing with them, or indeed with anybody; it springs from fountains as deep as those of character or religion. Now that between them they have got the Peerage practically by heart, its study, though they often read over favourite passages together, no longer takes them much time or conscious thought, it merely permeates them like Christianity or the moral qualities. It tinges all they do, and they do a great many very kind and considerate and generous things. Sir Baronet is the most liberal giver; no appeal made for a deserving and charitable object ever came to him in vain, but deep in his heart all the time that he is signing his munificent cheque, the thankful cries of the poor folk he has succoured sound in his ears, as they murmur, 'Thank you, Sir Baronet!' 'Bless you, Sir Baronet!' Lady Mary is equally open-handed, especially when children

25

and dumb animals are concerned, and she declares she can almost hear the thumping of the dogs' tails as they strive to say, 'Thank you, my lady!' 'Bless your ladyship's kind heart.'

Occasionally, out of mere exuberance, Sir Baronet sounds an insincere note. He wrote once to Oswald bidding him bring his wife to dinner in these terms: 'Bring my lady along to dinner on Tuesday week, my boy. No party, just ourselves, and I think the Princess told me the French Ambassador and the Duchess of Middlesex were to take their cutlets with us.'
. . . But all the time his pen was so trembling with gratification that for the moment Oswald thought his father must have a fit of shivering, till the truer explanation dawned on him, and he realized that the usually neat and careful handwriting was blurred with joy. But perhaps this little insincerity is but the mark of the most complete snob of all, who affects to make light of the attainments towards which his holiest and highest aspirations have been ever directed. Anyhow, one would be sorry to think that Sir Baronet was sincere over this, for it would imply that he was getting used to Ambassadors and Dukes, that he was becoming blasé with a surfeit of aristocracy. That would be too tragic a fate for so

thoroughly amiable an ass.

There is nothing more stimulating in this drab world than to look at those who intensely enjoy the prosperity which surrounds them, and to see Sir Baronet stepping along Piccadilly with his springy walk, and his ruddy face ready to be wreathed in smiles as he takes off his hat to some social star, is sufficient to reconcile the cynic and the disappointed, if they have any touch of humanity left in them, to a world where some people have such a wonderfully pleasant time. Perhaps if cynics were a little simpler, a little more alive to the possible joys of existence, they would share some of those raptures themselves. A princely fortune is no necessity to the snob: it is possible to taste his joys on a modest competence. But character and thoroughness are needful: he must read his Peerage till the glamour grows about the pages, and must value aright the little paragraphs in newspapers which record the doings of the mighty. Unless men are born with this gift, it is true they will not enter the highest circle of the Paradiso, but they should at least be able to leave the Inferno far below them. And as a matter of fact, most people have a touch (just a touch) of the snob innate in them, if they will only take the pains to look for it.

THE FREAKS OF MAYFAIR

They may not have the peerage-mind, but probably there is some sort of worldly success before which they are willing to truckle. It is worth a little trouble, in view of the spiritual reward, for the snob always has an aim in life : he never drifts along a purposeless existence.

The chronicler is tempted to linger a little over these happy and prosperous persons, and forecast the further glories that inevitably await them. At present a certain number of the Vere de Veres turn up their patrician noses when Marigolds are mentioned, which is exceedingly foolish of them, considering that it is out of Marigolds that the very best Vere de Veres have been made. The Marigolds will win eminence and renown by their industry, their riches, and their colossal respectability. That was how the Vere de Veres became the cream of the country, and instead of calling the Marigolds 'those tradesmen,' they would be wiser to hail them as cousins who will buttress up some of their own tottering lines (if their sons and daughters can only manage to marry into the Marigolds) by reinforcing them with their own vigorous blood, their wealth, and not least, their respectability. In the next generation Oswald Owen Vivian Lancelot will be Earl of Ballamuck and Viscount

THE COMPLEAT SNOBS

Marigold, and his children, of whom he has only eleven at present, will be Members of Parliament, and hard-working soldiers and diplomatists, with peeresses for sisters. When a few more years have rolled, the Vere de Veres will have to respect them, for they will be Vere de Veres, good, strong, honest Vere de Veres, the pick of the bunch, for with their healthy bodies, active brains, and, above all, their untarnished respectability, they are precisely the folk on whom honours pour down in spate. And what *is* the use of affecting to despise a family that in a hundred years will number bishops and ambassadors and generals among its collaterals, and will certainly have a family banner in St. George's Chapel?

AUNT GEORGIE
CHAPTER TWO

CHAPTER TWO
AUNT GEORGIE

AUNT GEORGIE'S CHRISTIAN name as bestowed by godparents with silver mugs at baptism was not Georgiana but simply George. He was in fact an infant of the male sex according to physical equipment, but it became perfectly obvious even when he was quite a little boy that he was quite a little girl. He played with dolls rather than lead soldiers, and cried when he was promoted to knickerbockers. These peculiarities, sad in one so young, caused his parents to send him to a boys' school at the early age of nine, where they hoped he might learn to take a truer view of himself. But this wider experience of life seemed but to confirm him in his delusions, for when he quarrelled with other young gentlemen, he did not hit them in the face with his fist, but slapped them with the open hand and pulled their hair. It was observed also that when he ran (which he did not like doing) he ran from the knees instead of striding from the hips. He did little, however, either in the way of running or of quarrelling, for he was of a sedentary and sentimental disposition, and formed a violent attachment to another young lady, on whom Nature

33

THE FREAKS OF MAYFAIR

had bestowed the frame of a male, and they gave each other pieces of their hair, which were duly returned to their real owners when they had tiffs, with inexorable notes similar to those by which people break off engagements. These estrangements were followed by rather oily reconciliations, in which they vowed eternal friendship again, treated each other to chocolates and more hair, and would probably have kissed each other if they had dared. Their unnatural sentiments were complicated by a streak of odious piety, and they were happiest when, encased in short surplices, they sang treble together in the school choir out of one hymn-book.

Public-school life checked the outward manifestation of girlhood, but Georgie's essential nature continued to develop in secret. Publicly he became more or less a male boy, but this was not because he was really growing into a male boy, but because through ridicule, contempt, and example he found it more convenient to behave like one. He did not like boys' games, but being tall and strong and well-made, and being forced to take part in them, he played them with considerable success. But he hated roughness and cold weather and mud, and his infant piety developed into a sort of sentimental rapture with stained-glass windows and ecclesiastical rites and church music. His public school was one where Confession to the Chaplain was, though not insisted on, encouraged, and Georgie conceived a sort of passion for this athletic young priest, and poured out to him week by week a farrago of pale and bloodless peccadilloes, and thought how wonderful he was. Eventually the embarrassed clergyman, who was of an ingenious turn of mind, but despaired of ever teaching Georgie manliness, invented a perfectly new penance for him, and forbade him to come to confession, unless he had really something desperate to say, more frequently than once every three weeks. Otherwise, apart from those religious flirtations, Georgie appeared to be growing up in an ordinary human manner. But, if anyone had been skilful enough to dissect him down to the marrow of his soul, he would have found that Georgie was not passing from boyhood into manhood, but from girlhood into womanhood.

He went up to Oxford, and there, under the sentimental influence of the city of spires, the last trace of his manhood left him. His father, who, by one of Nature's inimitable conjuring tricks, was a bluff old squire, rather too fond of port now, just as he had been rather too fond of the first line of the Gaiety Chorus in his youth, longed for Georgie to sow some wild oats, to get drunk or gated, to get entangled with a girl, to do anything to show that virility, though sadly latent, existed in him. But Georgie continued to disappoint those unedifying wishes: he preferred barley-water to port, and was always working in his room by ten in the evening, so that he would not have known whether he was gated or not, and he took no interest in any choruses apart from chapel choirs, and never got entangled with anybody. Instead he became a Roman Catholic, and a mixture of port, passion, and apoplexy carried off his father before he had time to alter his will.

Georgie stepped into his father's shoes, and continued his own blameless career. He had an income of some three thousand a year and a small place in Sussex, and at the conclusion of his Oxford days, turned over the place in Sussex to his step-mother and his three plain sisters, reserving there a couple of rooms for himself, and took a small neat house in Curzon Street. He was both generous and careful about money, made his sisters ample allowances, and proceeded to spend the rest of his income thoughtfully and methodically. He had an excellent taste in furniture and decorations, though an essentially feminine one, and the house in Curzon Street became a comfortable and charming little nest, with Chippendale furniture in the drawing-room and bottles of pink bath-salts with glass spoons in the bath-room. He had a private den of his own (though anything less like a den was never seen), with a looking-glass over the fire-place into which he stuck invitation-cards, a Chesterfield sofa, on the arm of which there often reposed a piece of embroidery, a writing-table with all sorts of dainty contrivances, such as a smelling-bottle, and a little piece of soft sponge in a dish, over the damp surface of which he drew postage-stamps instead of licking them with his tongue, and by degrees he got together a collection of carved jade, which was displayed in a *vitrine* (vulgarly, a glass case) lined with velvet and lit inside by electric light. He had a brougham motor-car, driven by a handsome young chauffeur, whom, if he took the wrong turning, he called a ' naughty boy ' through the tube, and was personally attended by a very smart young parlour-maid, for though he did not care for girls in any proper manly way, he liked, when he was sleepy in the morning, to

37

hear the rustle of skirts. His cook, whom he
saw every day after breakfast in his den, was an
artiste, and he had a good cellar of light wines.
After lunch and dinner he always made coffee
himself, in Turkish fashion, for his guests, and
passed round with it odd, syrupy liqueurs. His
bedroom was merely a woman's bedroom, with a
blue quilt on the bed, a long cheval-glass on the
floor, silver-backed brushes on the toilet-table
and no razors, for a neighbouring barber came
to shave him every morning. In cold weather,
when his mauve silk pyjamas were hung out to
warm in front of the fire, the parlour-maid in-
serted into his bed a hot-water bottle, jacketed
in the same tone of blue as his quilt. On that
Georgie put his soft pink feet, and always went
to sleep immediately.

Here he lived a kind and blameless life, but
the life of a sprightly widow of forty, who is rich
and childless, and does not intend to marry again.
In the morning, after seeing his cook, he wrote
a few letters (he did not use the telephone much
because it tickled his ear, and he disliked talking
into a little box where other people had talked
and breathed) and these he generally sealed with
a signet belonging to his step-mother's grand-
mother, which had a coronet on it. He was a

little snobbish in this regard, in a Victorian old-fashioned way, for though his step-mother was no sort of relation to him he took over her relations as cousins, and hunted up the most remote connections of hers, for adoption, in the Peerage. His letters being finished he took his soft hat and sat at his club for half an hour reading the papers. Generally he walked out to lunch, and was called for by his car about a quarter to three. Sometimes he had a little shopping to do, and if not, went for a drive, sitting very upright, much on the look-out for acquaintances, and returned home for tea. After tea he sat on his sofa working at his embroidery, had a hot bath, and, except when, about twice a week, he had a few people to dine with him, went out to dinner. He did not play bridge but patience and the piano, both of which he manipulated with a good deal of skill. When he entertained at his own house, his guests were chiefly young men with rather waggly walks and little jerky movements of their hands, and old ladies with whom he was always a great success, for he understood them so well. He called them all, young men and old ladies alike, 'my dear,' and they had great gossips together, and they often said Georgie was very wicked, which was a lie.

THE FREAKS OF MAYFAIR

He had considerable musical taste, as well as proficiency on the piano, and very soon his life became a busy one in the sense, at any rate, that he had very little time for his embroidery. He built out a big room at the back of his house, and gave tinkling little modern musical parties, at which he introduced masses of young geniuses to the notice of his friends. Also he took to practising his piano with some seriousness, and would often forgo his walk to the club and his perusal of the morning papers in order to work at his music, and sat at his instrument for two hours together, with his rings and his handkerchief on the candle-brackets. His taste was modern, and he liked the kind of piece about which you are not sure if it is over or not, or what has happened. He paid quantities of country-house visits to the homes of his old-lady friends and his step-mother's cousins, where he would sit in the library reading and writing his letters till half-past twelve, and take a little stroll with a brown cape on his arm till lunch-time. He sketched too, and produced rather messy water-colours of churches and beech-trees, and made crayon-portraits of his hostess or her boys, which he always sent her with his letter of thanks for a most pleasant visit, neatly framed. His por-

Aunt Georgie

traits of elderly ladies had a certain resemblance
to each other, being based on a formula of a lace
cap, a row of pearls, and a thoughtful expression. He had a similar formula for young men,
of which the chief ingredients were a cricket-
shirt and no coat or Adam's apple, long eye-
lashes, and a girlish mouth. He was not good at
eyes, so his sitters were always looking down.
After lunch at these most pleasant visits he went
out for a drive in a motor to see some neighbouring point of interest or to call on some adopted
cousin whom he had discovered to live somewhere about. He rested in his own room after
these fatigues and excitements for an hour before dinner, with his feet up and a dressing-gown
on, and afterwards would work on a crayon-
sketch, play the piano, or make himself agreeable to anybody who was in need of gentle conversation. Often he would settle down thus in
a friend's house for a fortnight at a time, in which
case he brought his embroidery and his car with
him, and was most useful in taking other guests
out for drives, or bringing home members of
a shooting-party. Occasionally, for no reason,
he roused violent antagonism in the breasts of
rude brainless men, and after he had left the
smoking-room in the evening, one would some-

times say to another, ' Good God! What is it?'

Georgie lived in this whirl of pleasant pursuits for some ten years. The only disagreeable incident that occurred during this time was that his attractive chauffeur married his attractive parlour-maid, and for a little, surrounded by hateful substitutes, he was quite miserable. But he wooed the selfish pair back again by taking a garage with a flat above it, where they could keep house, raising Bowles's wages, and getting in another parlour-maid when the curse of Eve was on Mrs. Bowles, and when he was now about thirty-five, Georgie definitely developed auntishness. As seen above, there were already many symptoms of it, but now the disease laid firm and incurable hold on him.

His auntishness was of the proverbial maiden-aunt variety, and was touched with a certain acid and cattish quality that now began to tinge his hitherto good-natured gossipy ways. As usually happens, he tended to detect in his friends and acquaintances the defects which he laboured under himself, and found that Cousin Betty was getting so ill-natured, and Cousin John had spoken most sarcastically and unkindly to him. His habits became engrained, and when he went out to dinner, as he continued to do, he took

42

with him a pair of goloshes in a brown paper parcel, if he meant to walk home, in case the crossings might be muddy. He was faithful enough to his old friends, the waggly-walking young men of his youth, and such of his old ladies who survived, and still went out with them on sketching-parties when they stayed together in the country, but otherwise he sought new friends among young men and young women, to whom he behaved in a rather disconcerting manner, sometimes, especially on sunny mornings, treating them like contemporaries, and wishing to enter into their 'fun,' sometimes petting them, as if they were children, and sometimes, as if they were naughty children, getting cross with them. He wanted in fact to be a girl still, and yet receive the deference due to a middle-aged woman, which is the *clou* to maiden-auntishness. He had little fits of belated and senile naughtiness, and would take a young man to the Gaiety, and encourage him to point out which of the girls seemed to him most attractive, and then scold him for his selfishness if he did not appear eager to come back home with him, and sit for an hour over the fire until Georgie felt inclined to go to bed. Or, having become a sort of recognised chaperone in London, he would take a girl-cousin (step-mother's side) to a ball, and be vexed with her because she had not had enough dancing by one o'clock. It must not be supposed that it was his habit to appear in so odious a light, but it sometimes happened. To do him justice, he was repentant for his ill-humour next day, and would arrange a little treat for a boy and a girl together, driving them down in his car to the Mid-Surrey golf-club, where they had a game, while he sat and sketched the blue-bells in Kew Gardens.

By this time his step-mother was dead (Georgie did a lovely crayon of her after death), and two out of his three plain sisters had married. The other used often to stay with him in London, and often he would bring quite a large party of young people down to the house in Sussex, where they had great romps. Georgie was quite at his best when entertaining in his own house, and he liked nothing better every now and then than a pillow-fight in the passage, when, emitting shrill screams of dismay and rapture, and clad in a discreet dressing-gown over his mauve silk pyjamas, he laughed himself speechless at the 'fun,' and bore the breakage of the glass of his water-colour pictures with the utmost good-humour. But when he had

44

had enough himself, he expected that everybody else should have had enough too, therein disclosing the fell features of Aunt Georgie.

Georgie did not, as the greyer seas of the forties and fifties began to engulf him, fall into the errors of grizzly kittens, but took quite kindly to spectacles when he wanted to read the paper or write his letters, and made no secret of his annual visit to Harrogate, to purge himself of the gouty tendencies which he had inherited from his father. He did not, of course, announce the fact that he had had a fresh supply of teeth, or that he had instructed his dentist to give a studied irregularity to them, and it is possible that he used a little hair-dye on his moustache which he clipped in the new fashion, leaving only two small tufts of hair like tails below his nostrils, but he quite dropped pillow-fights, though keeping up his music and his embroidery, and more than keeping up the increasing ill-nature of his tittle-tattle. He made great pets of his chauffeur's children, who in their artless way sometimes called him 'Daddy' or 'Grandpa.' He did not quite like either of these appellations, and their mother was instructed to impress on their infant minds that he was 'Mister Uncle Georgie.' But 'Miss

Auntie Georgie' would have been far more appropriate.

It is perhaps needless to add that he has never married and never will. Soon the second set of girl-friends whom he chose when he first developed auntishness will be middle-aged women, and as, since then, he has made quantities of new young friends, his table will never be destitute of slightly effeminate young men and old ladies. Those are the sections of humanity with whom he feels most at home, because he has most in common with them. He makes a fresh will about once every five years, leaving a good deal of his property to the reigning favourites, who are probably cousins (of his step-mother's). But most of them are cut out at the next revision, because they have shown themselves 'tarsome,' or in some way inconsiderate. But probably it will be a long time before anybody reaps the benefit of these provisions, for apart from his gout, which is kept in check by his visits to Harrogate, Georgie is a very healthy old lady. He lives a most wholesome life with his little walks and drives, and never, never has he committed any excesses of any sort. These very ageing things, the passions, have never vexed him, and he will no doubt outlive most of those who from time to time have been beneficiaries under his will.

After all he has done less harm than most people in the world, for no one ever heeded his gossip, and even if he has not done much good or made other people much happier, he has always been quite good and happy himself, for such malice as he impotently indulged in he much enjoyed, and he hurt nobody by it.

It would be a very cruel thing to think of sending poor Georgie to Hell ; but it must be confessed that, if he went to Heaven, he would make a very odd sort of angel.

QUACK-QUACK
CHAPTER THREE

CHAPTER THREE
QUACK-QUACK

UNDYING INTEREST IN THINGS abstruse, experimental, or charlatanish keeps Mrs. Weston perennially young. She has a small pink husband, who desires nothing more of life than to be allowed a room to himself, regular meals, a little walk after lunch followed by a nap at his club, and a quantity of morning and evening papers to read. Indeed it may be said of him that the morning and evening papers were his first day and will certainly be his last, for he is the sort of person who will die suddenly and quietly after dinner in his arm-chair. All those simple needs are easily supplied him, for when, for reasons to be subsequently mentioned, he cannot get regular meals at home he procures them at the Carlton grill-room.

The two have no children, and her husband being so simply provided for, Mrs. Weston has plenty of leisure to pursue her own weird life. She began, as most students of the faddish side of life do, by using her excellent physical health as a starting-point for hypochondria, and proceeded to cure herself of imaginary ailments with such ruthless ferocity that if she had not stopped in time, she might really have become

51

ill. As it was, she arrested her downward course of healing before it had done anything more than make her thin, and took to another fad. But she resumed her pleasant plumpness when she embraced spiritualism, for spiritualism for some obscure reason almost invariably causes people to lay on flesh.

To begin at the beginning of her quackings, she was about thirty when the shattering conviction came over her, after reading a little book about gout, that she entirely consisted of uric acid. This painful self-revelation caused her husband to become a regular habitué of the Carlton grill-room, for he was not strong enough to stand the ideal régime which blasted his once comfortable home. For a day or two he insisted on continuing his suicidal diet, but he found it impossible to enjoy his cutlet when his wife told him that all he ate turned the moment he had swallowed it, into waste products, and that his apparent appetite was merely the result of fermentation. Such news when he was at lunch quite spoiled his pleasure and stopped his fermentation. For herself, she proceeded to obtain body-building materials out of nuts and cheese, and calorics out of the oil with which she soaked the salads that were hoary with vegetable salts.

QUACK-QUACK

All tea and coffee were, of course, forbidden, since they reeked of purins, while if you drank anything at meals, you might just as well have a glass of prussic acid then and there, in order to get it over quicker. Probably if anyone had told her only to eat between meals, she would have tried that too. But all day the kitchen boiler rumbled with the ebullition of the oceans of hot water that had to be drunk in the middle of the morning and the middle of the afternoon, and before going to bed. It had to be sipped, and since at each sitting a quart or so must be lodged within her, the process was a lengthy one, and she could not get out of doors very much. But exercise and air were provided for by courses of stretchings and bendings and flickings and kickings done by an open window in front of a chart and a looking-glass, followed by spells of complete relaxation (which meant lying down on the floor). Then there were deep-breathing exercises, in which Mrs. Weston had to draw in her breath very slowly, hold it till she got purple in the face and the veins stood out like cords on her benignant forehead, and emit it all in one hurricane-puff. The dizziness and queer sensations that sometimes followed she took to be a proof of how much good it was doing her.

53

THE FREAKS OF MAYFAIR

Strange hungry-looking visitors used to arrive at queer hours, and talk to their enthralled pupil in an excited manner about arterio-sclerosis, and chromagens, and produce out of their pockets little packets of tough food, tasting of travelling-bags, which they masticated very thoroughly, and which in the space of a square inch contained the nutritive value of eight mutton chops and two large helpings of apple tart. Fortified by this they launched into the functions and derangements of the principal organs of the body, with an almost obscene wealth of detail, while Mrs. Weston used to sit in rapt attention to those sybils and long for dinner time to come in order that she might thwart her uric acid again.

She pursued her meatless course for several weeks with fanatic enthusiasm, and having been perfectly well before, found that, apart from a slight falling away of flesh, her iron constitution stood the strain remarkably well. Then while the nuts were yet in her mouth, so to speak, it struck her that she ought to go in for breathing exercises more thoroughly, and found that they led straight into the lap of the wisdom of the Yogis. This philosophy instantly claimed her whole attention, and she steeped herself in its manuals, and advertised in the *Morning Post*

54

for a Guru. An individual in a turban answered this in person, but as, after his second visit she found that a valuable ring was missing, which at his bidding she had taken off her finger in order to be less trammelled by material bonds, she decided to be her own Guru, and with the chapter on 'Postures' open before her, practised tying herself into knots. Her abstinence from meat came in useful, since a light diet was recommended by her new ideal in life, so also did her practice in deep-breathing, for Pranayama was entirely concerned with that, and when you had mastered Postures and Pranayama you would live in perfect health and vigour, as long as you chose. Again her superb physical health stood her in good stead, and she neither dislocated her limbs from Postures, nor had a single stroke of apoplexy from holding her breath. During the Yogi attack her husband ceased to take his meals at the Carlton grill-room, for he was allowed meat again in moderation. But he always used to go out for a walk when the great breathings began in the middle of the morning, since he hated the idea that in the next room Jane was sitting cross-legged on the floor, exhaling her long-held breath through one nostril while she closed the other with her finger, muttering 'Om! Om!' Long periods of absolute silence alternated with these mutterings, and it gave him an uncomfortable feeling to know that Jane was holding her breath all that time. Away from Chesterfield Street the image of her was less vivid, and when he returned for lunch Postures were over too, and though rather stiff and tired, she would declare that she never had known before what real health meant. This was always a pleasant hearing, and he would congratulate her on her convalescence, and instantly repent of his cordiality, because she urged him just to do a couple of Postures a day and see how he felt.

Then a misfortune which within a couple of days she temporarily called the turning-point of her life, befell Mrs. Weston, for she caught a chill (manifestly from posturing on a cold damp day in front of an open window) which indicated its presence by a simultaneous attack of lumbago and a streaming cold in the head. This latter made the inhalation of breath through the nostrils quite impossible, and the former, Postures. So shut out from the practice of Pranayama and Postures, she came winging it back from the East, and, happening to come across a copy of the *Christian Science Journal*, flew to the bosom

56

Queek - Queck

of Mrs. Eddy. Her only regret was that she had not left the heathen fold in time to frustrate the false claims of her indisposition, which had taken a firm and painful hold of her, but she had scarcely learned by heart the True Statement of Being when the severity of the symptoms began sensibly to diminish. In point of fact within three days she was perfectly well again, as she might have been all along if she had only known in time that there was no such thing as lumbago. Neither was there such a thing as uric acid or chromagens, and in consequence, since there was nothing to fear from disorders that had no existence, she ordered an excellent dinner that evening, and over ox-tail soup and fish and a roast pheasant, of all of which she ate heartily, she discoursed to her husband on the new truth that had risen like dawn over her previously benighted horizon. But, such is the ingratitude of man, he felt that he would sooner have eaten his dinner in silence at the grill-room than at home to the accompaniment of such preposterous harangues. And when, after dinner, just as he was settling down to a game of patience, Jane asked him to join with her in the recital of the True Statement of Being, he replied with some asperity that a True Statement of Balderdash was a fitter name for such nonsense.

Christian Science made Mrs. Weston brighter and younger and more robust than ever. Being quite convinced that there were no such things as discomfort or evil or disease or death, she recognised with increased vividness that the world was an exceedingly pleasant place, and went about all day with a brilliant smile. This smile became rather hard and fixed when small false claims put in their appearance, as, for instance, when a fish-bone seemingly stuck in her throat, or when, reciting the True Statement of Being as she went upstairs, she forgot the last step and tumbled rather heavily on to her knees. Thus, in the semblance of choking or of agonising pain in the knee-cap, it was necessary to tie the smile on, so to speak, lest the false claim should get a foothold. What made the house more uncomfortable for her husband was that his false claims were ignored also, so that if his study fire was found not to be lit, and the room in consequence like an ice-house, instead of sympathising with him over the carelessness of the housemaid, Jane continued to assure him that there was no such thing as cold, though her teeth were chattering in her head. She got into touch with other sufferers from these cheerful delusions, who seemed to him to resemble gargoyles with their fixed inflexible smiles, and their attitudes of determined hilarity, and the house became a perfect Bedlam of invincible cheerfulness, which was depressing to the last degree. He had a moment of reviving hope when Jane woke one morning with a very plausible claim in a wisdom-tooth, which the uninitiated would have called a raging toothache, and which he hoped might convince her. But learning, by telephone, from a healer that though the pain would certainly vanish with absent treatment, it was permissible to go to a dentist in order to save time, for mere manipulation (in other words having the tooth out), his hopes faded again. Mrs. Eddy herself, it appeared, had consulted a dentist in such circumstances, and Mrs. Weston did the same, and came home, brighter than ever, having had the tooth extracted quite painlessly under laughing-gas. The last thing she had said to herself, so she triumphantly announced, before she went off was that the extraction wouldn't hurt at all, and it didn't. The True Statement of Being had scored one triumph the more in completely annihilating not only the sense of pain, but common-sense also.

59

THE FREAKS OF MAYFAIR

Now the insidiousness of fads is that they are invariably based on something which is true and reasonable, and thus have an appeal to reasonable persons. In this they are unlike superstitions, for superstition is in its essence unreasonable, and Mrs. Weston would no more have bowed to the new moon (seen not through glass) or turned her money, than she would have been made miserable by breaking a looking-glass. She knew perfectly well that the fact of her seeing the new moon could not affect the prosperity of her investments, while if that amiable satellite had any power over her money it would certainly exercise it whether she curtsied or not. But her embrace of the vegetarian and Christian Science faith was undoubtedly based on reason: it was true that fleshless foods contained less uric acid than sirloin of beef: it was true also that if she or anybody else had a slight headache, that headache would in all probability efface itself quicker if she occupied herself in other matters, and, instead of sitting down to think about her headache denied it in principle by disregarding it. But it is easily possible to stretch a reasonable proposition too far, and make it applicable to things to which it does not apply, and it is exactly here that the faddist begins to differ from reasonable people. A sufficiently excruciating pain cannot be banished from the consciousness, and it is not the slightest use asserting that it does not exist. At this point, with regard to her wisdom-tooth, she became momentarily reasonable again, and had it out with laughing-gas like a sensible person. But then her mind rushed back again, like air into an exhausted receiver, into the vacuum of faddishness, and she became happier and more ridiculous than ever. The effect must never be denied: the faddist while convinced of her fad is extremely cheerful, as is natural to one who has found out and is putting in practice the secret of ideal existence. It made poor Mr. Weston very uncomfortable, but since one of the strongest characteristics of Christian Scientists is their inhuman disregard of other people, she did not take any notice of a little thing like that, and proceeded to make home unhappy with utter callousness.

But it was not her way to attach herself for very long to one creed: she flew, like a bee gathering honey from every flower, to suck the sweetness out of every fad, and presently she turned her volatile mind to the study of the unseen world that she suddenly felt to be sur-

rounding her. Christian Science no doubt had
its basis in the unseen, but in its application it
was chiefly concerned with bodily ailments and
discomforts, and the True Statement of Being
harnessed itself, so to speak, to a congested liver
or a sore throat. But now she went deeper yet,
and took the final plunge of the faddist and the
credulous into the sea of spiritualism.

Now in this highly organised city of London,
if you want anything you can always get on the
track of something of the sort by a few enquiries,
and one of Mrs. Weston's discarded vegetarians
introduced her to the celebrated medium, and
general fountain-head in the matters of table-
turning, crystal-gazing, automatic writing, ma-
terialisation, séances, planchettes and auras, the
Princess Spookoffski. Nobody could produce
positive proof that she was not a Russian Princess, for Russia is a very large place, and has
probably many princesses, nor that her companion, a small man with a chin-beard and a
positive passion for going into trances, was not
a Polish refugee of high birth. This august lady
was beginning to do very good business in town,
for London, ever Athenian in its desire for some
new thing, had just turned its mind to psychical
matters, and held séances with quenched lights

in the comfortable hour between tea and dinner, and had much helpful converse with the spirits of departed dear ones, and discarnate intelligences, that were not always remarkably intelligent.

Mrs. Weston accordingly went by appointment to the Princess's flat in a small street off Charing Cross Road, and was received by the Polish refugee of high birth, who conducted her through several small rooms, opening out of each other, to the presence of the sybil. These rooms had a lot of muslin draped about them, and were dimly lit with small oil lamps in front of shrines containing images or portraits hung with faded yellow jasmine of the great spiritual guides from Moses down to Madame Blavatsky, and a faint smell of incense and cigarettes hung about them. In the last of these the Princess was sitting lost in profound meditation. She wore a blue robe, serpents of yellow and probably precious metal writhed up her arm, and she had a fat pasty face with eyebrows so black and abundant as to be wholly incredible. Eventually she raised her head, and with a deep sigh fixed her beady eyes on Mrs. Weston. Then in a throaty voice she said:

'My child, you 'ave a purple 'alo.'

THE FREAKS OF MAYFAIR

This was very gratifying, especially when the Princess explained that only the most elect souls have purple halos, and the man with the chin-beard, whom the Princess called Gabriel dear, said that the moment he touched Mrs. Weston's hand he knew she had power. Thereupon the Princess's fingers began to twitch violently, and Gabriel dear, explaining that Raschia, the spirit of an ancient Egyptian priestess, possessed her, brought a writing-pad and a pencil, and the Princess, with Raschia to guide her, dashed off several pages of automatic script. This was written in curious broken English, and the Princess gaily explained that darling Raschia was not very good at English yet, for she was only learning. But the message was quite intelligible, and clearly stated that this new little friend, Mrs. Weston, was a being of the brightest psychical gifts, which must instantly be cultivated. It ended 'Ta, ta, darlings. Raschia must fly away. God bless you all.'

It was not to be wondered at that after so cordial a welcome, Mrs. Weston joined Princess Spookoffski's circle, and went there again next day for a regular séance, price two guineas a head. There were four other persons beside the Princess and Gabriel and they all had purple halos, for the Princess was so great an aristocrat in the spiritual world (as well as being a Princess on the mortal plane) that she only 'took' purple halos. The room swam with incense, a small musical-box was placed in the middle of the table, and hardly had the lights been put out and the circle made, when Gabriel, who was to be the medium, went off into a deep trance, as his stertorous breathing proved, and the musical-box began to play 'Lead, kindly Light.' On which the Princess said—

'Ah, perhaps the dear Cardinal will come to us. Let us all sing.'

Thereupon they all began helping the Cardinal to come by joining in to the best of their powers, with the gratifying result that before they were half-way through the second verse, a stentorian baritone suddenly joined in too, and that was the Cardinal singing his own hymn. He had a quantity of wholly edifying things to say when the hymn was over, such as ' beyond the darkness there is light,' and 'beyond death there is life,' and 'beyond trouble there is peace.' Having delivered himself of these illuminating truths, he said 'Good-bye, Benedictine, my children,' and left the mortal plane. Thereupon there was dead silence again, except for Gabriel's stertorous breathing.

A perfect tattoo of raps followed, and amid peals of spiritual laughter, Pocky announced that he was coming. Pocky was a dear naughty boy, the Princess explained to Mrs. Weston, so full of fun, and so mischievous, and had been, when on earth, a Hungarian violinist. Pocky's presence was soon announced by a shrill scream from the lady on Mrs. Weston's right, who said the naughty boy had given her such a slap. Then he pulled the Princess's hair, and a voice close to Mrs. Weston said ''Ullo, 'ullo, 'ere is a new friend. What a nice lady! Kiss me, ducky,' and Mrs. Weston distinctly felt a touch on her neck below her ear. Then after another bastinado of raps, Pocky's face, swathed in white muslin and faintly luminous, appeared above the middle of the table. They had had lovely music that day, he told them, 'on the other side,' and Pocky had played to them. If they all said 'please,' he would play to them now, and after they had all said 'please,' play to them he did on a violin. His tune was faintly reminiscent of a Brahms valse, but as it was a spirit air it could not have been that. Then with a clatter the violin descended on to the middle of the table, and Pocky, after blowing kisses to them all, went

66

away in peals of happy laughter.

Thereafter Mrs. Weston became a prey to psychical things. She gazed into the crystal she purchased from the Princess; she sat for hours, pencil in hand, waiting for automatic script to outline itself on her virgin paper; she took excursions into astrology; she frequented a fashionable palmist, who gave her the most gratifying information about her future, and assured her that marvellous happiness and success would attend her every step in life, so long as she regularly consulted Mrs. Jones, say once a week at seven and sixpence. The Princess and Gabriel gave a séance in Chesterfield Street, and put her into communication with her great-uncle, whose portrait by Lawrence happened to be hung in the hall. The Princess had been struck with this the moment she saw it, for the purpleness of the halo (even in the oil-picture) astonished her, and she asked who that saint was. He had not been recognised as such while on the earth, but no doubt he had learned much afterwards, for his remarks at the séance that evening equalled Cardinal Newman's for spiritual beauty. To clinch the matter, he materialised at the next séance, and apart from his nose, which certainly did resemble Gabriel's, his great-niece found that he exactly corresponded with her childish remembrances of him.

For several months these spiritual experiences were a source of great happiness to Mrs. Weston, but, though encouraged to persevere, she could never see anything in her crystal except the distorted reflection of the room, nor would Raschia do anything in the way of automatic script except cover the paper with angled lines which resembled fortifications. Similarly at the séances, Pocky and Uncle Robert and Cardinal Newman did not seem to get on, but remained on their respective levels of mischievousness and saintliness, without any further revelations. Her attendances became less frequent and her crystal grew dusty from disuse, while she found that whether she consulted Mrs. Jones or not, her life moved forward on a quite prosperous course. But fortunately about this time she encountered a disciple of the Higher Thought, and soared away again into the bright zenith of another enthusiasm, which still at present holds her.

She is one of the happiest freaks in all Mayfair, with never a dull or a despondent moment. The limits of a normal lifetime are not large enough to allow her to exhaust all the quackeries with

QUACK-QUACK

which from time immemorial the inquisitive sons of men have deluded and delighted themselves, and if she lives till ninety, which is quite probable, she will continue to find fresh outlets for her exuberant credulity. Just now she finds that Higher Thought is much assisted by walking with bare feet through wet grass for a quarter of an hour every morning. The only sufficiently private grass in London is a small sooty patch in her own back-garden. But it is grass, and it is usually wet in the early morning, and she has her bath afterwards.

THE POISON OF ASPS
CHAPTER FOUR

Poison of Asps.

CHAPTER FOUR
THE POISON OF ASPS

HORACE CAMPBELL HAS AN UN-
erring gift of smudging whatever he speaks of.
As he speaks most of the time, he manages to
smudge a good deal, and in consequence is in
great demand at somewhat smudgy houses by
reason of his appropriate and amusing conversation. Every decent man would like to kick him,
and every nice woman would like to slap his fat
white face, and so his habitats are the establish-
ments of those not so foolishly particular. But
though he lunches and dines without intermis-
sion at other people's houses, he is in no degree
one who sings for his dinner, for he has a quite
distinct career of his own, and spends his mornings earning not daily bread only, but truffles
and asparagus and all the more expensive foods,
by teaching other people to sing. His knowledge of voice-production is quite unrivalled,
and he could probably, if he chose, turn a corn-
crake into a contralto. The enormous fees that
he charges thus enable him to compress into
three hours the period of his working day, and
during that time he is the father and mother of
most of the beautiful noises that next year will
be heard rising from human throats at concerts

and opera-houses. Then, his business being over and his pocket fat, he puts on his black morning coat, and his cloth-topped shoes, his grey silk tie with the pearl tie-pin, and goes forth to cause himself as well as his pocket to grow fat, and makes a music of his own.

Now his thesis, his working hypothesis, the basis of his conversation, is this. There are always several possible causes which may account for all that happens in the busy little world of London, and in discussing such happenings, he invariably assumes the smudgiest and more scandalous cause. A few instances will make this clear.

Example (1): John Smith is engaged to Eliza Jones.

Possible causes:

(i.) John Smith loves Eliza Jones and Eliza Jones loves John Smith.

(ii.) John Smith is after Eliza Jones's money.

(iii.) It was high time that John Smith *did* marry Eliza Jones.

Of these possible causes Horace Campbel leaves cause (i.) out of the question as not worth consideration. Cause (ii.) may account for it, but he invariably prefers cause (iii.).

Or again—

THE POISON OF ASPS

Example (2): Mrs. Snookes went to the opera with Mr. Snookes.

Probable causes:

(i.) Husband and wife went to the opera because they like going to the opera.

(ii.) Mrs. Snookes has an affair with the famous tenor Signor Topnotari.

(iii.) Mr. Snookes is paid £2 : 2 : 0 a night to applaud the soprano Signora Beeinalt.

It is idle to point out which cause Horace Campbell proceeds to discuss.

Example (3): An eminent statesman goes into the country for a week-end.

Possible causes:

(i.) The eminent statesman needs rest.

(ii.) 'Somebody' goes with him.

Horace Campbell's law of causation again applies.

Here then is the postulate which lies at the root of his conversation, his standpoint towards life. He does not bear ill-will towards those on whose conduct he habitually places the worst conceivable motive, and he has no political or personal objection to the eminent statesman, whom he would be very glad to know: it is merely that a nasty thing perches on his mind with greater facility than a nice one, and evokes greater sympathy there. Scandalous innuendoes seem to him more amusing than innocent interpretations, and so too, it appears, do they seem to those at whose tables he makes himself so entertaining. His stories are considered 'too killing,' whereas there is nothing very killing about the notion that Mr. and Mrs. Snookes went to the opera because they liked music. Also he has a perfect command of the French language, and often for the sake of guileless butlers and footmen he tells his little histories in French, which produces an impression of intrigue and wit in itself. Love-affairs, the theme round which he revolves, are no doubt of perennial human interest, but he has but little sympathy with a love-affair founded on or culminating in marriage. It must have some taint of the illicit to be worth his busy embroidering needle; the other has a touch of the bourgeois about it. Suggestiveness is more to his mind than statement, hints than assertions. To judge by his conversation you would think that he and the world generally swam in fathomless oceans of vice, but as far as conduct goes, he never swam a stroke. At the utmost he took off his shoes and stockings, and paddled at the extreme edge of that unprofitable sea. He just pruriently paddles there with his fat white feet. . . .

It has been said that every decent man would like to kick him, but in justice to him it must be added that he is not nearly so unkindly disposed towards anybody. Decent men, like such bourgeois emotions as honest straightforward love, only bore him, and he merely yawns in their faces. But though he has no direct malice, no desire to injure anyone by his *petites saletés*, he has, it must be confessed, a grudge against all those whom he considers collectively as being at the top of the tree. He has enough brains to know that the majority of the class Mr. and Mrs. Not-quite-in-it, who are his intimate circle, have not a quarter of his cleverness, but what he has not brains to see is that the very gifts of belittlement and scandal-scattering that make him such a tremendous success with them, are exactly the gifts which prevent his being welcomed in more desirable circles. It would be altogether beyond the mark to hint that he is in any way under a cloud: at the most he is, like the cuttlefish, enveloped in an obscurity of his own making. Though perfectly honest himself, he would certainly, if anyone remarked that honesty was the best policy, retort that successful swindling was at least a good second, and it is exactly that habit of mind that causes him to be *planté là*, as he would say himself, among the Not-quite-in-its. Humour, of which he has plenty, is no doubt the salt of life, but all his humour has gone rancid. It is there all right, but it has gone bad, and gives a healthy digestion aches. But flies settle on it, and are none the worse. Though there is no direct malice in him towards those against whom he so incessantly uses his little toy tar-squirt, there is a distinct trait of jealousy, that one vice that is quite barren of pleasure, for of all the commandments there is none except the tenth the breaking of which does not bring to the transgressor some momentary gratification. That, too, accounts in large measure for the raptures he causes at the tables of the Not-quite-in-its, for they, like him, yearn to be quite in it, and not being able to manage it, applaud this dainty use of the tar-squirt against those who are. They have plenty of money, plenty of brains, plenty of artistic tastes, and they would certainly scream with laughter if they were told that it was just the want of a very bourgeois quality, namely good-nature, that bars the fulfilment of their just desires. Yet such is the case: they are not 'kind inside.' They are (ever so slightly) pleased at other people's checks and set-backs, and herein in the main consists their second-rateness.

Horace Campbell is perhaps the priest of this little nest of asps, and without doubt the priestess is the amazing Mrs. Dealtry, now flaming in the sunset of her witty discontented life. She is tall and corpulent, with wonderful vitality and quantities of auburn hair and carmine lip salve, and mauve scarves, and when she and Horace Campbell get together, as they do two or three times a day, to discuss their friends, those who die, so to speak, and are dismissed by them, are the lucky ones, for the rest they drive with whips through the London streets, without a rag of reputation to cover them. She, like Horace, has plenty of humour, and if the sight of a wrinkled old woman with a painted face, and one high-heeled foot in the grave, dealing out horrible innuendoes like a pack of cards, does not make you feel sick, you will enjoy her conversation very much. Years ago she started the theory that Horace was devotedly attached to her, and for her sake committed celibacy, and though she has changed her friends more often than she changes her dress, she still sticks to the gratifying belief that she has wrecked his life.

' Horace might have done anything,' she is

accustomed to say, 'but he would always waste his time on me. Poor Horace! such a dear, isn't he, but how much aged in this last year or two. And I can't think why somebody doesn't tell him to have his teeth attended to.'

Then as Horace entered the room she made a place for him on the sofa.

'Monster, come here at once,' she said. 'Now what is the truth about Lady Genge's sudden disappearance? I am told he simply turned her out of the house, which any decent man would have done years ago.'

'He did,' said Horace, 'and she always came in again by the back door. This time he has turned her out of the back door. On dit que "Cherchez le valet."'

Mrs. Dealtry gave a little scream of laughter.

'Last time it was the girl's music master,' she said. 'She will never take servants with a character.'

'Character for what?' asked Horace. 'Sobriety?'

'She was at the opera three nights ago, but blind drunk, though you mustn't repeat that. I'm told she had her tiara upside down with the points over her forehead. Alice Chignonette, as I call her, was with her, a small horse-hair bun

80

glued with seccotine to the back of her head. She hadn't got any clothes on, but was slightly distempered.'

'She always is slightly distempered, except when she holds four aces and four queens, and has seen the whole of her opponent's hand so that she knows whether to finesse or not. And is it true that the Weasel has stopped her allowance?'

'Yes, he gave her a coat of dyed rabbit-skins with a card *pour prendre congé*, and a second-class ticket to Milwaukee where he first found her on the sidewalkee. What people get into society now! Large bare shoulders, a perpetual cold in the head and the manners of a Yahoo are a sufficient passport. One can't go anywhere without running into them. Not a soul would speak to her at Milwaukee so she came to London for whitewash.'

'And distemper.'

'She brought that with her. The Weasel carried it in his grip-sack.'

Horace took an enamelled cigarette-case out of his pocket and lit a cigarette that smelt of musk.

'I saw Lily Broomsgrove to-day,' he said. 'She has become slightly broader than she is long.'

'Her conversation always was. It consists of seven improper adjectives and one expletive. That is why she is so popular. She can be easily understood.'

'She seemed to have an understanding with Pip Rippington. He was enclosed.'

'He ought to be. Haven't you heard? That golf club he started, you know. Apparently golf was a terminological inexactitude. I suppose it will all be common property soon, so I may as well tell you.'

Mrs. Dealtry proceeded to tell them, and all the little asps hissed with pleasure. . . .

Now there was very little truth in all that Mrs. Dealtry had been saying, and perhaps none at all in Horace Campbell's contribution, yet while each of them really knew the other was a liar, each drank it all in with the utmost avidity. Such malice as there was about them was completely impotent malice: it could not possibly matter to Pip Rippington, for instance, whoever he was, that Mrs. Dealtry and Horace had been inventing stories about him. That he had founded a golf club was perfectly true; that Mrs. Dealtry had not been welcomed as a member of it was true also, though there was a needless *suppressio*

82

veri about this fact, as everybody present was perfectly aware of it. But it amused them in some rancid manner to vent spleen, just as it perhaps amuses asps to bite. Only, and here was one of Time's revenges, nobody ever cared what either of them said. To throw mud enough is proverbially supposed to ensure the sticking of some of it, but in the case of them and those like them, the proverb was falsified. They had said that sort of thing too often and too emphatically for any one to attach the smallest importance to it; it was as if their victims had been inoculated for the poison of asps, and suffered no subsequent inconvenience from the bite. No one thought of bringing the laws about libel into play over them, any more than people think about invoking the protection of those laws against a taxi-driver who compensates himself in compliments for the tip he has not received. If they have any sense they get themselves into their houses and leave the vituperative driver outside. That is just what decent people did with Horace Campbell. He is outside still, biting the paving-stones.

The pity of it all is the appalling waste among asps of brains, inventive faculty, and humour. If only their gifts were used to some laudable or even only innocent purpose, the world in general would gain a great deal of entertainment, and the asps of the popularity and success that they secretly crave for. As it is, some sort of moral ptomaine has infected them, some invasion of microbes that turns their wit into poison. Whatsoever things are loathsome, whatsoever things are of ill report, they think of those things. All their wit, too, goes to waste: nobody cares two straws what they say, and the bitten are pathetically unconscious of having received any injury whatever. That fact, perhaps, if they could thoroughly realise it, might draw their fangs.

THE SEA-GREEN
INCORRUPTIBLE
CHAPTER FIVE

CHAPTER FIVE
THE SEA-GREEN
INCORRUPTIBLE

CONSTANCE LADY WHITTLEMERE lives in a huge gloomy house in the very centre of Mayfair, has a majestic appearance, and is perfectly ready for the Day of Judgment to come whenever it likes. From the time when she learned French in the school-room (she talks it with a certain sonorous air, as if she was preaching a sermon in a cathedral) and played Diabelli's celebrated duet in D with the same gifted instructress, she has always done her duty in every state of life. If she sat down to think, she could not hit upon any point in which she has not invariably behaved like a Christian and a lady (particularly a lady). Yet she is not exactly Pharisaical; she never enumerates even in her own mind her manifold excellences, simply because they are so much a matter of course with her. And that is precisely why she is so perfectly hopeless. She expects it of herself to do her duty, and behave as a lady should behave, and she never has the smallest misgiving as to her complete success in living up to this ideal. That being so, she does not give it another thought, knowing quite well that, whoever else may do doubtful or disagreeable things, Constance Whittlemere will move undeviatingly on in her flawless courses, just as the moon, without any diminution of her light and serenity, looks down on slums or battle-fields, strewn with the corpses of the morally or physically slain. And Lady Whittlemere, like the moon, does not even think of saying, 'Poor things!' She is much too lunar.

At the age of twenty-two (to trace her distressing history) her mother informed her, at the close of her fourth irreproachable London season, that she was going to marry Lord Whittlemere. She was very glad to hear it, for he was completely congenial to her, though, even if she had been very sorry to hear it, her sense of duty would probably have led her to do as she was told. But having committed that final act of filial obedience, she realised that she had a duty to perform to herself in the person of the new Lady Whittlemere, and climbed up on to a lofty four-square pedestal of her own. Her duty towards herself was as imperative as her duty towards Miss Green had been, when she learned the Diabelli duet in D, and was no doubt derived from the sense of position that she, as her husband's wife, enjoyed. Yet perhaps she hardly

88

SEA-GREEN INCORRUPTIBLE

'enjoyed' it, for it was not in her nature to enjoy anything. She had a perfectly clear idea, as always, of what her own sense of fitness entailed on her, and she did it rigidly. 'The Thing,' in fact, was her rule in life. Just as it was The Thing to obey her governess, and obey her mother, so, when she blossomed out into wifehood, The Thing was to be a perfect and complete Lady Whittlemere. Success, as always, attended her conscientious realisation of this. Luckily (or unluckily, since her hope of salvation was thereby utterly forfeited) she had married a husband whose general attitude towards life, whose sense of duty and hidebound instincts equalled her own, and they lived together, after that literal solemnisation of holy matrimony in St. Peter's, Eaton Square, for thirty-four years in unbroken harmony. They both of them had an unassailable sense of their own dignity, never disagreed on any topic under the sun, and saw grow up round them a copious family of plain, solid sons and comely daughters, none of whom caused their parents a single moment's salutary anxiety. The three daughters, amply dowried, got married into stiff mahogany families at an early age, and the sons continued to prop up the conservative interests of the nation by becoming severally (i.) a soldier, (ii.) a clergyman, (iii.) a member of Parliament, (iv.) a diplomatist, and they took into all these liberal walks of life the traditions and proprieties of genuine Whittlemeres. They were all Honourables, and all honourable, and all dull, and all completely conscious of who they were. Nothing could have been nicer.

For these thirty-four years, then, Lady Whittlemere and her husband lived together in harmony and exquisite expensive pomposity. Had Genesis been one of the prophetical books, their existence might be considered as adumbrated by that of Adam and Eve in the Garden of Eden. Only there was no serpent of any kind, and their great house in shelter of the Wiltshire downs had probably a far pleasanter climate than that of Mesopotamia. Their sons grew up plain but strong, they all got into the cricket Eleven at Eton, and had no queer cranky leanings towards vegetarianism like Abel, or to homicide like Cain, while the daughters until the time of their mahogany marriages grew daily more expert in the knowledge of how to be Whittlemeres. Three months of the year they spent in London, three more in their large property in the Highlands of Scotland, and the

SEA-GREEN INCORRUPTIBLE

remaining six were devoted to Home Life at Whittlemere, where the hunting season and the shooting season with their large solid parties ushered in the Old English Christmas, and were succeeded by the quietness of Lent. Then after Easter the whole household, from major-domo to steward's-room boy, went second-class to London, while for two days Lord and Lady Whittlemere 'picnicked' as they called it at Whittlemere, with only his lordship's valet and her ladyship's maid, and the third and fourth footmen, and the first kitchen-maid and the still-room maid and one housemaid to supply their wants, and made their state entry in the train of their establishment to Whittlemere House, Belgrave Square, where they spent May, June, and July.

But while they were in the country no distraction consequent on hunting or shooting parties diverted them from their mission in life, which was to behave like Whittlemeres. About two hundred and thirty years ago, it is true, a certain Lord Whittlemere had had 'passages,' so to speak, with a female who was not Lady Whittlemere, but since then the whole efforts of the family had been devoted to wiping out this deplorable lapse. Wet or fine, hunting and shooting notwithstanding, Lord Whittlemere gave audience every Thursday to his estate-manager, who laid before him accounts and submitted reports. Nothing diverted him from his duty, any more than it did from distributing the honours of his shooting lunches among the big farmer-tenants of the neighbourhood. There was a regular cycle of these, and duly Lord Whittlemere with his guests lunched (the lunch in its entirety being brought out in hampers from The House) at Farmer Jones's, and Farmer Smith's, and Farmer Robertson's, complimented Mrs. Jones, Smith, and Robertson on the neatness of their gardens and the rosy-facedness of their children, and gave them each a pheasant or a hare. Similarly whatever Highnesses and Duchesses were staying at The House, Lady Whittlemere went every Wednesday morning to the Mothers' Meeting at the Vicarage, and every Thursday afternoon to pay a call in rotation on three of the lodgekeepers' and tenants' wives. This did not bore her in the least : nothing in the cold shape of duty ever bored her. Conjointly they went to church on Sunday morning, where Lord Whittlemere stood up before the service began and prayed into his hat, subsequently reading the lessons, and

SEA-GREEN INCORRUPTIBLE

giving a sovereign into the plate, while Lady Whittlemere, after a choir practice on Saturday afternoon, played the organ. It was the custom for the congregation to wait in their pews till they had left the church, exactly as if it was in honour of Lord and Lady Whittlemere that they had assembled here. This impression was borne out by the fact that as The Family walked down the aisle the congregation rose to their feet. Only the footman who was on duty that day preceded their exit, and he held the door of the landau open until Lady Whittlemere and three daughters had got in. Lord Whittlemere and such sons as were present then took off their hats to their wife, mother, sisters and daughters and strode home across the Park.

And as if this was not enough propriety for one day, every Sunday evening the vicar of the parish came to dine with the family, directly after evening service. He was bidden to come straight back from evensong without dressing, and in order to make him quite comfortable Lord Whittlemere never dressed on Sunday evening, and made a point of reading the *Guardian* and the *Church Family Newspaper* in the interval between tea and dinner, so as to be able to initiate Sabbatical subjects. This fortunate

93

clergyman was permitted to say grace both before and after meat, and Lord Whittlemere always thanked him for 'looking in on us.' To crown all he invariably sent him two pheasants and a hare during the month of November and an immense cinnamon turkey at Christmas.

In this way Constance Whittlemere's married life was just the flower of her maiden bud. The same sense of duty as had inspired her school-room days presided like some wooden-eyed Juggernaut over her wifehood, and all her freedom from any sort of worry or anxiety for these thirty-four years served but to give her a shell to her soul. She became rounded and water-tight, she got to be embedded in the jelly of comfort and security and curtseying lodge-keepers' wives, and 'yes-my-lady'-Sunday-Schools. Such rudiments of humanity as she might possibly have once been possessed of shrivelled like a devitalised nut-kernel, and, when at the end of these thirty-four years her husband died, she was already too proper, too shell-bound to be human any longer. Naturally his death was an extremely satisfactory sort of death, and there was no sudden stroke, nor any catching of vulgar disease. He had a bad cold on Saturday, and, with a rising temperature, in-

94

sisted on going to church on Sunday. Not content with that, in the pursuance of perfect duty he went to the stables, as usual, on Sunday afternoon, and fed his hunters with lumps of sugar and carrots. It is true that he sent the second footman down to the church about the time of evensong, to say that he was exceedingly unwell, and would have to forgo the pleasure of having Mr. Armine to dinner, but the damage was already done. He developed pneumonia, lingered a decorous week, and then succumbed. All was extremely proper.

It is idle to pretend that his wife felt any sense of desolation, for she was impervious to everything except dignity. But she decided to call herself Constance Lady Whittlemere, rather than adopt the ugly name of Dowager. There was a magnificent funeral, and she was left very well off.

Le Roi est mort: Vive le Roi : Captain Lord Whittlemere took the reins of government into his feudal grasp, and his mother with four rows of pearls for her life, two carriages and a pair of carriage horses and a jointure of £6000 a year entered into the most characteristic phase of her existence. She was fifty-six years old, and since she proposed to live till at least eighty, she bought the lease of a great chocolate-coloured house in Mayfair with thirty years to run, for it would be very tiresome to have to turn out at the age of seventy-nine. As befitted her station, it was very large and gloomy and dignified, and had five best spare bedrooms, which was just five more than she needed, since she never asked anybody to stay with her except her children's governess, poor Miss Lyall, for whom a dressing-room was far more suitable : Miss Lyall would certainly be more used to a small room than a large one. She came originally to help Lady Whittlemere to keep her promise as set forth in the *Morning Post* to answer the letters of condolence that had poured in upon her in her bereavement, but before that gigantic task was over, Lady Whittlemere had determined to give her a permanent home here, in other words, to secure for herself someone who was duly conscious of the greatness of Whittlemeres and would read to her or talk to her, drive with her, and fetch and carry for her. She did not propose to give Miss Lyall any remuneration for her services, as is usual in the case of a companion, for it was surely remuneration enough to provide her with a comfortable home and all found, while Miss Lyall's own property of £100 a year would amply clothe her, and enable her to lay something by. Lady Whittlemere thought that everybody should lay something by, even if, like herself, nothing but the total extinction of the British Empire would deprive her of the certainty of having £6000 a year as long as she lived. But thrift being a duty, she found that £5000 a year enabled her to procure every comfort and luxury that her limited imagination could suggest to her, and instead of spending the remaining £1000 a year on charity or things she did not want, she laid it by. Miss Lyall, in the same way could be neat and tidy on £50 a year, and lay by £50 more.

For a year of mourning Constance Whittlemere lived in the greatest seclusion, and when that year was out she continued to do so. She spent Christmas at her son's house, where there was always a pompous family gathering, and stayed for a fortnight at Easter in a hotel at Hastings for the sake of sea-breezes. She spent August in Scotland, again with her son, and September at Buxton, where further to fortify her perfect health, she drank waters and went for two walks a day with Miss Lyall, whose hotel bills she, of course, was answerable for.

97

THE FREAKS OF MAYFAIR

Miss Lyall similarly accompanied her to Hastings, but was left behind in London at Christmas and during August.

A large establishment was of course necessary in order to maintain the Whittlemere tradition. Half-a-dozen times in the season Lady Whittlemere had a dinner-party which assembled at eight, and broke up with the utmost punctuality at half-past ten, but otherwise the two ladies were almost invariably alone at breakfast, lunch, tea, and dinner. But a cook, a kitchen-maid, and a scullery-maid were indispensable to prepare those meals, a still-room maid to provide cakes and rolls for tea and breakfast, a butler and two footmen to serve them, a lady's maid to look after Lady Whittlemere, a steward's-room boy to wait on the cook, the butler, and the lady's maid, two housemaids to dust and tidy, a coachman to drive Lady Whittlemere, and a groom and a stable-boy to look after the horses and carriages. It was impossible to do with less, and thus fourteen lives were spent in maintaining the Whittlemere dignity downstairs, and Miss Lyall did the same upstairs. With such an establishment Lady Whittlemere felt that she was enabled to do her duty to herself, and keep the flag of tradition flying.

98

SEA-GREEN INCORRUPTIBLE

But the merest tyro in dignity could see that this could not be done with fewer upholders, and sometimes Lady Whittlemere had grave doubts whether she ought not to have a hall-boy as well. One of the footmen or the butler of course opened the front-door as she went in and out, and the hall-boy with a quantity of buttons would stand up as she passed him with fixed set face, and then presumably sit down again.

The hours of the day were mapped out with a regularity borrowed from the orbits of the stars. At half-past nine precisely Lady Whittlemere entered the dining-room where Miss Lyall was waiting for her, and extended to her companion the tips of four cool fingers. Breakfast was eaten mostly in silence, and if there were any letters for her (there usually were not) Lady Whittlemere read them, and as soon as breakfast was over answered them. After these literary labours were accomplished, Miss Lyall read items from the *Morning Post* aloud, omitting the leading articles but going conscientiously through the smaller paragraphs. Often Lady Whittlemere would stop her. 'Lady Cammerham is back in town is she?' she would say. 'She was a Miss Pulton, a distant cousin of my husband's. Yes, Miss Lyall?'

THE FREAKS OF MAYFAIR

This reading of the paper lasted till eleven, at which hour, if fine, the two ladies walked in the Green Park till half-past. If wet, they looked out of the window to see if it was going to clear. At half-past eleven the landau was announced (shut if wet, open if fine), and they drove round and round and round and round the Park till one. At one they returned and retired till half-past, when the butler and two footmen gave them lunch. At lunch the butler said, 'Any orders for the carriage, my lady?' and every day Lady Whittlemere said, 'The victoria at half-past two. Is there anywhere particular you would like to go, Miss Lyall?' Miss Lyall always tried to summon up her courage at this, and say that she would like to go to the Zoological Gardens. She had done so once, but that had not been a great success, for Lady Whittlemere had thought the animals very strange and rude. So since then she always replied:

'No, I think not, thank you, Lady Whittlemere.'

They invariably drove for two hours in the summer and for an hour and a half in the winter, and this change of hours began when Lady Whittlemere came back from Harrogate at the end of September, and from Hastings after

SEA-GREEN INCORRUPTIBLE

Easter. Little was said during the drive, it being enough for Lady Whittlemere to sit very straight up in her seat and look loftily about her, so that any chance passer-by who knew her by sight would be aware that she was behaving as befitted Constance Lady Whittlemere. Opposite her, not by her side, sat poor Miss Lyall, ready with a parasol or a fur boa or a cape or something in case her patroness felt cold, while on the box beside Brendon the coachman sat the other footman, who had not been out round and round and round the Park in the morning, and so in the afternoon went down Piccadilly and up Regent Street and through Portland Place and round and round Regent's Park, and looked on to the back of the two fat lolloping horses which also had not been out that morning. There they all went, the horses and Brendon and William and Miss Lyall in attendance on Constance Lady Whittlemere, as dreary and pompous and expensive and joyless a carriage-load as could be seen in all London, with the exception, possibly, of Black Maria.

They returned home in time for Miss Lyall to skim through the evening paper aloud, and then had the tea with the cakes and the scones from the still-room. After tea Miss Lyall read for two hours some book from the circulating library, while Lady Whittlemere did wool work. These gloomy tapestries were made into screens and chair-seats and cushions, and annually one (the one begun in the middle of November) was solemnly presented to Miss Lyall on the day that Lady Whittlemere went out of town for Christmas. And annually she said:

'Oh, thank you, Lady Whittlemere; is it really for me?'

It was: and she was permitted to have it mounted as she chose at her own expense.

At 7.15 P.M. a sonorous gong echoed through the house; Miss Lyall finished the sentence she was reading, and Lady Whittlemere put her needle into her work, and said it was time to dress. At dinner, though both were teetotallers, wine was offered them by the butler, and they both refused it, and course after course was presented to them by the two footmen in white stockings and Whittlemere livery and cotton gloves. Port also was put on the table with dessert, this being the bottle which had been opened at the last dinner-party, and when Lady Whittlemere had eaten a gingerbread and drunk half a glass of water they went, not into the morning-room which they had used during the day, but the large drawing-room upstairs with the Louis Seize furniture and the cut-glass chandeliers. Every evening it was all ablaze with lights, and the fire roared up the chimney : the tables were bright with flowers, and rows of chairs were set against the wall. Majestically Lady Whittlemere marches into it, followed by Miss Lyall, and there she plays patience till 10.30 while Miss Lyall looks on with sycophantic congratulations at her success, and murmured sympathy if the cards are unkind. At 10.30 Branksome the butler throws open the door and a footman brings in a tray of lemonade and biscuits. This refreshment is invariably refused by both ladies, and at eleven the house is dark.

Now the foregoing catalogue of events accurately describes Lady Whittlemere's day, and in it is comprised the sum of the material that makes up her mental life. But it is all enacted in front of the background that she is Lady Whittlemere. The sight of the London streets, with their million comedies and tragedies, arouses in her no sympathetic or human current : all she knows is that Lady Whittlemere is driving down Piccadilly. When the almond blossom comes out in Regent's Park, and the grass is yellow with the flowering of the spring bulbs,

103

her heart never dances with the daffodils; all that happens is that Lady Whittlemere sees that they are there. She subscribes to no charities, for she is aware that her husband left her this ample jointure for herself, and she spends such part of it as she does not save on herself, on her food and her house and her horses and the fifteen people whose business it is to make her quite comfortable. She has no regrets and no longings, because she has always lived perfectly correctly, and does not want anything. She is totally without friends or enemies, and she is never surprised or enthusiastic or vexed. About six times a year, on the day preceding one of her dinners, Miss Lyall does not read aloud after tea, but puts the names of her guests on pieces of cardboard, and makes a map of the table, while the evening she leaves London for Hastings or Scotland she stops playing patience at ten, in order to get a good long night before her journey. She does the same on her arrival in town again so as to get a good long night after her journey. She takes no interest in politics, music, drama, or pictures, but goes to the private view of the Academy as May comes round, because The Thing recommends it. And when she comes to die, the life-long consciousness of

The Sea-Green Incorruptible.

SEA-GREEN INCORRUPTIBLE

The Thing will enable her to meet the King of Terrors with fortitude and composure. He will not frighten her at all.

And what on earth will the Recording Angel find to write in his book about her? He cannot put down all those drives round the Park, and all those games of patience, and really there is nothing else to say. . . .

THE ETERNALLY
UNCOMPROMISED
CHAPTER SIX

CHAPTER SIX
THE ETERNALLY UN-
COMPROMISED

WINIFRED AMES WAS THE YOUNG-est of a family of six girls, none of whom an industrious mother had managed to foist on to incautious husbands. They were all plain and square and strong (like carpets of extra width), and when seated at the family table in Warwick Square with their large firm mother at one end and a mild diminutive father at the other, resembled a Non-Commissioned Officers' mess. But Winifred was an anomaly, a freak in this array of stalwart maidenhood: there was something pretty about her, and, no less marked a difference between her and her sisters, something distinctly silly about her. Florence and Mary and Diana and Jane and Queenie were all silent and swarthy and sensible, Winifred alone in this barrack of a house represented the lighter side of life. A secret sympathy perhaps existed between her and her father, but they had little opportunity to conspire, for he was packed off to the City immediately after breakfast, and on his return given his dinner, and subsequently a pack of cards to play patience with.

THE ETERNALLY

She had a certain faculty of imagination, and her feathery little brains were constantly and secretly occupied in weaving exotic and sentimental romances round herself. If in her walks she received the casual homage of a stare from a passer-by in the street, she flamed with unsubstantial surmises. Positively there was nothing too silly for her; if the passer-by was shabby and disordered she saw in him an eccentric millionaire or a mysterious baronet, casting glances of respectful adoration at her; if he was well-dressed and pleasant to the eye she saw—well, she saw another one. There would be a wild and fevered courtship, at the end of which, in a mist of rice and wedding-bells, she would enter the magnificent Rolls-Royce and drive away, a lady of title, between the lines of the guard of honour furnished by her unfortunate sisters.

She kept these lurid imaginings strictly to herself, aware that neither Florence nor Mary nor Diana nor Jane nor Queenie would extend a sympathetic hearing to them. As far as that went she was sensible enough, for her imagination, lurid as it was, was right in anticipating a very flat and stern reception for them if she confided them to her sisters. But since she never ran the risk of having them dispersed by homely laughter, her day-dreams became more and more real to her, and at the age of twenty-two she was, in a word, silly enough for anything.

Then the amazing thing happened. A real baronet, a concrete, middle-aged, wealthy, delicate baronet who was accustomed to dine at the Non-Commissioned Officers' mess once or twice in the season, proposed to her, and it appeared that all her imaginings had not been so silly after all. She accepted him without the smallest hesitation, feeling that 'faith had vanished into sight.' Besides, her mother was quite firm on the subject.

Sir Gilbert Falcon (such was his prodigious name) was a hypochondriac of perfectly amiable disposition, and his Winny-pinny, as he fatuously called her, was at first extremely contented. He treated her like a toy, when he was well enough to pay any attention to her ; and in the manner of a little girl with her doll, he loved dressing her up in silks and jewels, with an admiration that was half child-like, half senile, and completely unmanly. It pleased his vanity that he, a little, withered, greenish man, should have secured so young and pretty a wife, and finding that green suited her, gave her his best

jade necklace, the beads of which were perfectly matched, and represented years of patient
collecting. He gave her also for her lifelong
adornment the famous Falcon pearls, which
pleased her much more. She wore the jade by
day, and the pearls in the evening, and he would
totter after her, when he felt well enough, into
the Rolls-Royce (for the Rolls-Royce had come
true also) and take her to dine at the Savoy.
Afterwards, when he had drunk his tonic, which
he had brought with him in a little bottle, he
often felt sufficiently robust to go on to a revue,
where he took a box. There he would sit, with a
shawl wrapped round his knees, and hold her
hand, and tell her that none of the little ladies
on the stage were half so enchanting as his
Winny-pinny.

Of course he could not indulge in such de-
bauches every night, and the evenings were
many when they dined at home and he went to
bed at half-past nine. Then when he was warmly
tucked up with a hot-water bottle and an eider-
down quilt, he would like her to sit with him, and
read to him till he got drowsy. Then he would
say, 'I'm getting near Snooze-land, Winny: shall
we just talk a little, until you see me dropping
off? And then, my dear, if you want to go out to

some ball or party, by all means go, and dance away. Such a strong little Winny-pinny to dance all night, and be a little sunbeam all day—' And his wrinkled eyelids would close, and his mouth fall open, and he would begin to snore. On which his Winny-pinny gently got up, and after shading the light from the bed, left the room.

At first she was vastly contented. Being a quite unreal little creature herself, it seemed delicious that her husband should call her his fairy and his Winny-pinny and his sunbeam, and only require of her little caresses and butterfly-kisses and squeezes. All the secret sentimental imaginings of her girlhood seemed to be translated into actual life; the world was very much on the lines of the day-dreams she had never ventured to tell her sisters. But by degrees fresh horizons opened, and her imagination, reinforced by continuous reading of all the sentimental trash that she could find in circulating libraries, began to frame all sorts of new adventures for herself. Just as, in her girlhood, she had had visions of baronets and millionaires casting glances of hopeless adoration at her in the streets, so now, when she had got her baronet all right, she still clung to the idea of others looking at her with eyes of silent longing. She decided (in a strictly imaginative sense) to have a lover who pined for her.

Now with her pretty meaningless face, pink and white, with her large china-blue eyes, and yellow hair, it was but natural that there were many men who looked with interest and admiration at her, and were very well content to sit and talk to her in secluded corners at the balls to which she so often went alone. After a few days' indecision she settled that the hopeless and pining swain (for she was determined to be a faithful wife, that being part of the romance) should be Joe Bailey, a pale and willowy young soldier, who spent most of the day at the manicurist and most of the night in London ball-rooms. From the first time she had seen him, so she now told herself, having adopted him as her lover, she had known that there was some secret sympathy between them; a chord (this came out of the circulating library) vibrated between their two souls. His pallor was instantly accounted for, so too was the tenderness with which he held her hand when they danced together: in spite of his noble reticence his soul had betrayed its secret to her.

After a week or two of noble reticence on his part, she came to the conclusion that she must also pine for him, else there would be no nobility in her fixed determination to be faithful to her husband. She flattered herself that she was getting on nicely with this, when the most dreadful thing happened, for Joe Bailey became engaged to somebody quite different, a real live girl with a great appetite, whose vocabulary was chiefly confined to the word 'top-hole.' Winifred herself was 'top-hole,' so was Joe Bailey, so were dogs, golfin' and dancin'. Anything that was not 'top-hole' was 'beastly.'

This was very disconcerting, and seeking safety in numbers Winifred decided to have quantities of lovers, for it was not likely that they should all go and marry somebody else. To ensure greater security she included in her list several married men, who had met her too late. Thus amply provided, she plunged into a new set of adventures.

The situation thus created was truly thrilling, and the thrill was augmented by amorous little sallies on her husband's part. His nerve tonic suited him, and about this time he used often to go out to dinner with her, and even come on for an hour to a ball, where he sat in a corner, feeding his vitality with the sight of all the youth and energy that whirled in front of him. He liked

seeing his Winny-pinny enjoy herself, and gave
little squeals of delight when he saw her dancing
(her dancing was really admirable) with a series
of vigorous young men. Then as they drove
away together (for when he went to a ball with
her, she had to come away with him) he would
squeeze her hand and say:

'Who was that last young man my Winny-
pinny danced with? And who was it in the dance
before who looked at her so fondly? And who
was it she sat out with all that time? But her old
man was watching her: oh, he had his eye on
her!'

Here then was the thrill of thrills in the new
situation. Gilbert had noticed how many men
were in love with her. And before long she
added to herself the almost inevitable corollary,
'Gilbert is so terribly jealous.'

But in spite of Gilbert's terrible jealousy, and
the suffocating crowds of lovers, nothing particular happened. The lovers all remained nobly
reticent, and a fresh desire entered her circul-
ating-library soul. She must get talked about:
people other than Gilbert must notice the fatal
spell that she exercised broadcast over the
adoring males of London: she must get compromised, somehow or other she must get

UNCOMPROMISED

compromised.

According to the circulating library there was nothing easier. A note with a few passionate words addressed to her had only to be picked up by somebody else's wife, or somebody else's husband had only to be found on his knees at midnight in her boudoir (a word she affected) and the thing was done. But, as always, it was the *premier pas qui coûte*, and these enchanting situations, she supposed, had to be led up to. A total stranger would not go on his knees at midnight in her boudoir, or leave passionate notes about; she had to rouse in another the emotion on which were built those heavenly summits, and begin, so to speak, in the valleys.

At this point a wonderful piece of luck came her way. The faithless Joe Bailey had his engagement broken off. It was generally supposed that the top-hole girl found him beastly, but Winifred knew better. She felt convinced that he had broken it off on her account, finding that passionate celibacy was the only possible condition for one who had met her too late. Here was an avenue down which compromise might enter, and when in answer to a broad hint of hers, he asked her to play golf with him at Richmond, she eagerly consented.

117

The plan was that he should lunch with Sir
Gilbert and herself, and Sir Gilbert held out
hopes that if it was not too hot, he would drive
down with them, sit on the verandah, or perhaps
walk a hole or two with them, and drive back
again at the conclusion of their game. But these
hopes were shattered or—should it be said—
more exciting hopes were gloriously mended,
for an inspection of the thermometer convinced
him that it would be more prudent to stay in-
doors till the heat of the day waned. So she
and Joe Bailey drove off together in the Rolls-
Royce.

She looked anxiously round as they left the
door in Grosvenor Square.

'I wonder if it was wise of us to come in this
car,' she said, timidly.

Bailey looked critically round.

'Why not,' he said rather stupidly. 'Quite
a good car, isn't it?'

Clearly he was not awake to the danger.

'Oh, yes,' she said, 'but people are so ill-
natured. They might think it odd for you and
me to be driving about in Gilbert's car.'

He was still odiously obtuse.

'Well, they couldn't expect us to walk all the
way to Richmond, could they?' he said.

UNCOMPROMISED

To her great delight, Winifred saw at this moment a cousin of her husband's, and bowed and waved her hand and kissed her fingers. She sat very much back as she did this so that Florrie Falcon, who had a proverbially unkind tongue, could clearly see the young man who sat by her side. That made her feel a little better, for it was even more important that other people should see her in the act of doing compromising things, than that he with whom she compromised herself should be aware of the fact. During their game again they came across several people whom Bailey or she knew, who, it was to be hoped, would mention the fact that they had been seen together.

It was a distinct disappointment to poor Winifred that this daring escapade seemed to have attracted so little notice, but she did not despair. A further glorious opportunity turned up indeed only a day or two later, for her husband was threatened with what he called a bronchial catarrh (more usually known as a cough) and departed post-haste to spend a couple of days at Brighton. Winifred, so it happened, was rather full of engagements, and he readily fell in with her wish to stop in town, and not to accompany him. So, the moment she had ceased kissing her finger-tips to him as he drove away in the Rolls-Royce with all the windows hermetically closed, she ran back into the house, and planned a daring scheme. She telephoned to Lady Buckhampton's, where she was dining and dancing that night, to say her husband had this tiresome bronchial catarrh, and that she was going down to Brighton with him, and, while the words were scarcely spoken, telephoned to Joe Bailey asking him to dine with her. He accepted, suggesting that they should go to the first-night at the Criterion after dinner, and then go on to the Buckhamptons' dance.

A perfect orgy of compromising situations swam before her, more thrilling even than the famous kneeling scene in her boudoir at midnight. She would go to the Criterion with her unsuspecting lover, where certainly there would be many people who would go on to the Buckhampton dance afterwards. They would all have seen her and Joe Bailey together, and even if they did not, he in the babble of ball-room conversation would doubtless popularise the fact of their having been there together. He might even tell Lady Buckhampton, whose invitation, on the plea of absence at Brighton with her husband, she had excused herself from, about this daring adventure.

The mere material performance of this evening came up to the brilliance of its promise. All sorts of people saw her and her companion, and the play happening by divine fitness to be concerned with a hero who backed out of his engagement at the last moment because he loved somebody else, Winifred could scarcely be expected not to turn blue eyes that swam with sympathy on her poor Joe. But again this hopeless young man did not understand, and whispered to know if she wanted sixpenny-worth of opera-glasses. He saw her home—this she had not contemplated—and sat with her in the barren boudoir, smoking a cigarette. Surely now he would slide on to his knees? But he did not, and went to his ball. There he actually told Lady Buckhampton that he had dined and been to the play with Lady Falcon, and she only laughed and said, 'Dear little Winny! She told me some nonsense about going to Brighton with her husband. How-de-*do*? *How*-de-do? So nice of you to have come.'

Then it is true Winny almost despaired of this particular lover. She made one more frantic effort when she met him next day at lunch, and said, 'You must talk to your neighbour more. People will notice,' but this only had the effect of making him talk to his neighbour, which was not what she meant.

She decided to give another lover a chance, and selected Herbert Ashton, a somewhat older man, who no doubt would understand her better. Several encouraging circumstances happened here, for her husband more than once remarked on the frequency with which he came to the house, and she thought one day that Lady Buckhampton cut her in the Park. This joy, it is true, was of short duration, for Lady Buckhampton asked her to spend the week-end with them next day, and she was forced to conclude that the cut had not been an intentional one. But it stimulated her to imagine a very touching scene in which Herbert, when they were alone together in the boudoir, was to say, 'This is killing me,' and fold her in his arms. For one moment she would yield to his fervent embrace, the next she would pluck herself from him and say, 'Herbert, I am a married woman: we met too late!' On which he would answer, 'Forgive me, my dearest: I behaved like a cad.'

And then the most dreadful thing of all happened, for part, at any rate, of her imaginings came true. She was with Herbert shortly afterwards in her boudoir, and in ordinary decent response to a quantity of little sighs and glances and glances away and affinity-gabble on her part, he had given her a good sound proper kiss. But it was real; it was as different as possible from all the tawdry tinsel sentimentalities which she had for years indulged in, and it simply terrified her. She gave one little squeal, and instead of yielding for a moment to his fervent embrace, and saying, 'Herbert, I am a married woman, etc.,' cried, 'Oh, Mr. Ashton!' which was very bald.

He looked at her completely puzzled. He felt certain she meant him to kiss her, and had done so.

'I'm sorry,' he said, 'I thought you wouldn't mind.'

A dreadful silence overcharged with bathos followed. Then recovering herself a little, she remembered her part.

'You must go now,' she said faintly, with a timid glance that was meant to convey the struggle she was going through. But unfortunately he only said 'Right oh,' and went.

Since that day she has always retreated in time to prevent anything real occurring. But she cannot succeed in getting talked about in

123

connection with anybody. The instinct of London generally, often at fault, is here perfectly correct. She can't be compromised—no one will believe anything against a woman so mild. And all the time, in the clutch of her sentimental temperament, she sees herself the heroine of great romances. Lately she has been reading Dante (in a translation) and feels that England lacks someone like the mighty Florentine poet, for his Beatrice is waiting for him. . . .

It is all rather sad for poor Winny-pinny. It is as if she desired the rainbow that hangs athwart the thundercloud. But ever, as faint yet pursuing she attempts to approach, it recedes with equal speed. Indeed, it is receding faster than she pursues now, for her hair is getting to be of dimmer gold, and the skin at the outer corners of those poor eyes, ever looking out for unreal lovers, is beginning faintly to suggest the aspect of a muddy lane, when a flock of sheep have walked over it, leaving it trodden and dinted.

THE GRIZZLY KITTENS
CHAPTER SEVEN

CHAPTER SEVEN
THE GRIZZLY KITTENS

A FOUNT OF PERENNIAL YOUTH-
fulness has been and will be the blessing and
curse of certain people's existence. Up to the
age of about thirty-five for a woman and round
about forty for a man, it is an admirable thing to
feel that the morning of life is still lingering in
rosy cloudlets about you, but when these austere
ages have been arrived at, it is wiser for those
who still behave like imperishable children to
recollect, impossible though they will find the
realisation of it without exercising patience and
determination, that, though their immortal souls
are doubtless imperishable, they are no longer
boys and girls. Otherwise the dreadful fate of
becoming grizzly kittens will soon lay ambushes
for them, and to be a grizzly kitten does not
produce at all the same impression as being an
imperishable child. Like Erin in the song and
King David in the psalm, they should remember
and consider the days of old, and attempt quietly
and constantly to do a little subtraction sum,
whereby they will ascertain how far the days
of old have receded from them. Their spring-
tide has ebbed a long way since then: they are
swimming in it no longer, they are not even

127

THE FREAKS OF MAYFAIR

paddling, but they are standing just a little gaunt and skinny high up on the beach, with wisps of dry sea-weed whistling round their emaciated ankles. Almost invariably those threatened with grizzly kittenhood are spare and thin, for this fact encourages the pathetic delusion that they have youthful figures, and in a dim light, to eyes that are losing their early pitilessness of vision they doubtless seem slim and youthful to themselves, though they rarely present this appearance to each other. But it is very uncommon to find a stout grizzly kitten: amplitude makes it impossible to skip about, and cannot be so readily mistaken by its hopeful possessors for youthful slimness.

Imperishable children, who are threatened with grizzly kittenhood, are, like other children and kittens, male and female. At this stage great indulgence must be extended to them whichever their sex may be, for their error is based upon vitality, which, however misapplied, is in itself the most attractive quality in the world. That they have no sense of time is in comparison a smaller consideration. For they are always cheerful, always optimistic, and if, at the age of forty, they have a slight tendency to say that events of twenty years ago are

THE GRIZZLY KITTENS

shrouded in the mists of childhood and the nursery, this is but an amiable failing, and one that is far easier to overlook than many of the more angular virtues. Of the two the female grizzly kitten (in the early stages of the complaint) is entitled to greater kindliness than her grizzly brother, for the obvious reason that in the fair of Mayfair the merry-go-round and the joy-wheel slow down for women sooner than they do for men. Thus the temptation to a woman of behaving as if it was not slowing down, is greater than to a man. It will go on longer for him ; he has less excuse—since he has had a longer joy-ride—for pretending that it is still quite at its height of revolving giddiness. She—if she is gifted with the amazing vitality which animates grizzly kittens—can hardly help still screaming and clapping her hands and changing hats, when first the hurdy-gurdy and the whirling begin to slacken, in order to persuade herself that they are doing nothing of the sort. If she is wise, she will of course slip off the joy-wheel and, like Mr. Wordsworth, 'only find strength in what remains behind.' But if she did that, the danger of her grizzly kittenhood would be over. Pity her then, when first the slowing-down process begins, but give less pity to the man who will not

129

accept the comparatively kinder burden of his middle-age. Besides, when the early stages of grizzly kittenhood are past, the woman who still clings to her skippings and her rheumatic antics after blind-tassels has so much the harder gymnastics to perform.

Two sad concrete examples of grizzly-kittenhood, both in advanced stages, await our commiseration. Mrs. Begum (née Adeline Armstrong) is the first. From her childhood the world conspired to make a grizzly kitten of her, and in direct contravention of the expressed wishes of her godfather and godmother who said she was to be Adeline, insisted on calling her Baby. Baby Armstrong she accordingly remained until the age of twenty-five, when she became Baby Begum, and she has never got further from that odious appellation, at her present age of fifty-two, than being known as Babs, while even now her mother, herself the grizzliest of all existing kittens, calls her Baby still.

Babs appeared in Mayfair at the age of seventeen, and instantly took the town by storm, in virtue of her authentic and audacious vitality. She had the face of a Sir Joshua Reynolds angel, the figure of a Botticelli one, the tongue of a *gamin*, and the spirits of an everlasting carnival.

THE GRIZZLY KITTENS

Her laugh, the very sound of that delicious enjoyment, set the drawing-room in a roar, and her conversation the smoking-room, where she was quite at home—there was never anyone so complete as she, never such an apple of attractiveness, of which all could have a slice. She would ride in the Row of a morning, call the policeman, who wanted to take her name on the score of excessive velocity, 'Arthur dear,' and remind him how she had danced in the cause of police old-age pensions at Clerkenwell (which was perfectly true), thus melting his austere heart. Then, as like as not, she would get off her horse at the far end of the ladies' mile, and put on it an exhausted governess, with orders to the groom to see her safe home to Bayswater. Then she would sit on the rail, ask a passer-by for a cigarette, and hold a little court of adorers, male and female alike, until her horse came back again. She would, in rare intervals of fatigue, go to bed about four o'clock in the morning, when her mother was giving a ball in Prince's Gate, and stand on the balcony outside her bedroom in her nightgown, and talk to the remaining guests as they left the house, shrieking good wishes, and blowing kisses. Or if the fit so took her, instead of going to bed she would change

131

her ball-dress for a riding-habit, go down to the mews with Charlie or Tommy or Harry, or indeed with Bertha or Florrie or Madge (fitting these latter up with other habits) and start for a ride in the break of the summer morning, returning hungry and dewy to breakfast. Whereever she went the world laughed with her; she enhaloed all she shone upon. Chiefly did she shine upon Charlie Gordon, who, in the measure of a man, was a like comet to herself. He was some five years older than she, and they expected to marry each other when the fun became less fast and furious. In the interval, among other things, they had a swimming-race across the Serpentine one early August morning, and she won by two lengths. An angry Humane Society boat jabbed at them with hooks in order to rescue them. These they evaded.

Those whom Nature threatens with grizzly kittenhood live too much on the surface to be able to spare much energy for such engrossing habits as falling in love, and when, at the age of twenty-five she suddenly determined to marry the small and silent Mr. Begum, nobody was surprised and many applauded. She could not go on swimming the Serpentine with Charlie Gordon, and it seemed equally unimaginable that

she should marry a man with only £2000 a year
and no prospects of any sort or kind. She did
not imperatively want him, any more than he imperatively wanted her, and since that one conclu-
sive reason for matrimony was absent, it did not
particularly matter whom she married, so long
as he was immensely wealthy, and of an indulgent temper. By nationality, Mr. Begum owed
about equal debts to Palestine, Poland, and
the Barbados, and since at this epoch Palestine
at any rate was in the ascendant over the roofs
of Mayfair it was thought highly suitable that
Baby Armstrong should become Baby Begum.
She had always called Charlie Gordon, 'dear,'
or 'darling,' or 'fool,' and she explained it all to
him in the most illuminating manner.

'Darling, you quite understand, don't you?'
she said, as she rode beside him one morning in
the Park. 'Jehoshaphat's a perfect dear, and he
suits me. Life isn't all beer and skittles, otherwise I would buy some beer, and you would save
up to get a second-hand skittle alley, and there
we should be! My dear, do look at that thing on
the chestnut coming down this way. Is it a goat
or isn't it? I think it's a goat. Oh don't be a fool,
dear, you needn't be a fool. Of course everybody thought we were going to marry each other,

but what can matter less than what everybody thinks? And besides, I know quite well that you haven't the slightest intention of getting broken-hearted about me, and the only thing you mind about is that I have shown I have not got a broken heart about you. What really is of importance is what I am to call Jehoshaphat. I can't call him Jehu, because he doesn't do anything furiously, and I can't call him "Fat," because he's thin, and there's nothing left!'

'I should call him "darling," then,' said Charlie, who was still unconvinced by this flagrant philosophy, 'same as you call me.'

She looked at him almost regretfully.

'Oh, do be sensible,' she said. 'I know I'm right: I feel I'm right. Get another girl. There are lots of them, you know.'

Charlie had the most admirable temper.

'I'll take your advice,' he said. 'And, anyhow, I wish you the best of luck. I hope you'll be rippingly happy. Come on, let's have a gallop.'

Since then, years, as impatient novelists so often inform us, passed. Babs's philosophy of life was excellent as far as it went, and the only objection to it was that it did not go far enough. In spite of his vitality, Charlie did not, as a

sensible young man should, see about getting
another girl; for perhaps he was wounded a little
deeper than either he or Babs knew. The tragedy about it all is that they both had the constitution of grizzly kittens. He did not marry any
one else, nor did he live into his age as that
slowly increased upon him, and Mr. Begum got
asthma. This made him very tiresome and
wheezy, and the perpetual contact with senility
probably prevented Babs from growing into her
proper mould of increasing years. Her sense
of youth was constantly fed by her husband's
venerable habits; with him she always felt a
girl. And the ruthless decades proceeded in
their Juggernaut march, without her ever seeing the toppling car that now overhangs her,
stiff with the wooden images of age. Wooden, at
any rate, they will seem to her when she fully per-
ceives them, and robbed of the graciousness and
wisdom that might have clothed and softened
them if only she had admitted their advent.

As it is, two pathetic figures confront us.
Charlie Gordon, that slim entrancing youth, is
just as slim (in fact slimmer in the wrong places)
as he ever was. But he is a shade less entrancing, with his mincing entry into the assembling
party than he was twenty-five years ago. There

was no need for him to mince then, for his eager
footsteps carried him, as with Hermes-heels, on
the wings of youth. Now he takes little quick
steps, and thinks it is the same thing. He is just
as light and spry as ever (except when he is
troubled with lumbago) but he cannot see that
it is not the same thing. He has not noticed that
his lean youthful jaw has a queer little fold in the
side of it, and if he notices it, he thinks it is a
dimple. He brushes his hair very carefully now,
not knowing that to the disinterested observer
the top of his head looks rather like music-paper,
with white gaps in between the lines, and that
it is quite obvious that he grows those thinning
locks very long on one side of his head (just
above the ear) and trains them in the manner of
an espaliered pear over the denuded bone where
once a plume used jauntily to erect itself. He is
careful about them now, but once, not so very
long ago, he forgot how delicately trained were
those tresses, and went down to bathe with the
other boys of the house. They naturally came
detached from their proper place, and streamed
after him as he swam, like the locks of a Rhine-
maiden. It was rather terrible. But such as they
are, they are still glossy raven black : there is not
the smallest hint of grey anywhere about them.

The Grisly Kitten.

THE GRIZZLY KITTENS

Again, once in days of old he had quick staccato little movements of his head, like some young wild animal, which suited the swiftness of his mercurial gambollings very well; to this day that particular habit has persisted, but the effect of it somehow is dismally changed; it is galvanic and vaguely suggests St. Vitus's abominable dance. He still jumps about with joy when he is pleased, but those skippings resemble rather the antics of a marionette than coltish friskings. He feels young, at least he has that quenchless appetite for pleasure that is characteristic of the young, but he isn't young, and his tragedy, the rôle of the grizzly kitten, stares him in the face. Perhaps he will never perceive it himself, and go on as usual, slightly less agile owing to the increasing stiffness of his venerable joints, until the days of his sojourning here are ended. Or perhaps he will see it, and after a rather depressing week or or two turn into a perfectly charming old man with a bald head and spectacles and a jolly laugh.

Mrs. Begum's fate hangs in the balance also. She has begun to think it rather daring of her to go larking about with a boy who is easily young enough to be her son, whereas in the days when such manœuvres were rather daring she never gave two thoughts to them. She still likes (or pretends to like) sitting up to the end of a ball, not in the least realising how appalling a spectacle she presents in the light of a June dawn. She can easily be persuaded to tuck up her skirts and dance the tango or the fox-trot or whatever it is that engages the attention of the next generation, and if she wants to sit down, she is as likely as not to flop cross-legged on the floor, or to perch herself on a friend's knee, with a cigarette in one hand and a glass of champagne cup in the other, and tell slightly risky stories, such as amused the partners of her youth. But for all her wavings of her wand, the spell does not work nowadays, and when poor Babs begins to be naughty, it is kinder of her friends to go away. Kitten-like she jumps at the blind-tassel still, but it is weary, heavy work, and she creaks, she creaks. . . .

But the most degrading exhibition of all is when Babs and Charlie get together. Then in order to show, each to each, that time writes no wrinkles on their azure brows, they give a miserable display of mature skittishness. They see which of them can scream loudest, laugh most, eat most, drink most, romp most, and, in

a word, be grizzliest. Their manner of speech
has not changed in the smallest degree in the
lapse of thirty years, and to the young people
about it sounds like some strange and outlandish tongue such as was current in the reign
of the second George. They are always betraying themselves, too, by whistling 'Two Lovely
Black Eyes' or some ditty belonging to the
dark ages, and to correct themselves pretend
that their mother taught it them when she came
to kiss them good-night in their cribs. They
do not deceive anybody else by their jumpings,
they do not deceive each other, and perhaps
they do not deceive themselves. But it is as if
a curse was on them: they have got to be dewy
and Maylike: if Charlie wants a book from the
far end of the room he runs to get it; when they
go into dinner together they probably slide
along the parquet floor. He is a little deaf, and
pretending to hear all that is said, makes the
most idiotic replies; and she is a little blind,
and cannot possibly read the papers without
spectacles, which she altogether refuses to wear.
If only they had married each other thirty years
ago they would probably have mellowed a little,
or at least could have told each other how ridiculous they were being. As it is, they both have

139

to screw themselves up to the key of the time when they swam the Serpentine together. Poor dear old frauds, why do they try to wrench themselves up to concert pitch still? Such a concert pitch! such strainings and bat-like squeaks! It would be so much better to get a little flat and fluffy, on the grounds of greater comfort to themselves, not to mention motives of humanity to others. For, indeed, they are rather a ghastly sight, dabbing and squawking at each other on the sofa, in memory of days long ago. The young folk only wonder who those 'funny old buffers' are, and they wonder even more when the funny old buffers insist on joining in a game of fives on the billiard-table, and the room resounds with bony noises as their hands hit the flying ball. But they scream in earnest then, because it does really hurt them very much. And then Mr. Begum gets wheeled in in his invalid chair with his rugs and his foot-warmers, and insists on talking to Charlie Gordon when the game is over (and his hands feel as if they had been bastinadoed), as if he was really an elderly man, and can remember the Franco-German war, which of course he can. But Charlie, though he stoutly denies the imputation, feels very uncomfortable, and changes the subject at the earliest opportunity. By this time Babs will have organised a game of rounders or something violent in the garden, in order to show that she is young too. She is getting very nut-crackery, and looks tired and haggard, as indeed she is. But she shouts to her husband, who is much deafer than Charlie, 'Daddy, darling, we're going to play rounders! Would you like to come out, or do you think it will be rather cold for you? Perhaps you'd be wiser not to. You won't play, I suppose, Charlie?'

And Charlie, nursing his bruised hands, says, 'Rounders? Bless me, yes. I'm not quite past rounders yet. Nothing like a good run-about game to keep you fit.'

It keeps him so fit that he is compelled to have a good stiff brandy and soda afterwards, to tone him up for the exertion of having dinner.

Wearily, aching in every limb, they creep into their respective beds. There seems to be a pillow-fight going on somewhere at the end of the passage, with really young voices shrieking, and the swift pad of light feet. Babs thinks of joining it, but her fingers fall from the pillow she has caught up, and she gets into bed instead, thinking she will be up to anything after a good night. And she would be up to anything that

THE FREAKS OF MAYFAIR

could decently be required of her, if only she would not present her grim and dauntless figure at such excursions. Already Charlie is dropping into a sleep of utter prostration: he wants to be in good trim to-morrow. There he lies with his thin Rhine-maiden hair reposing on his pillow. But he wakes easily, though slightly deaf, and at the first rattle of his door-handle when his valet calls him next morning he will instinctively gather it up over his poor bald pate.

And they might both be so comfortable and jolly and suitable. There is a wounding pathos about them both.

CLIMBERS:
I. THE HORIZONTAL
CHAPTER EIGHT

CHAPTER EIGHT
CLIMBERS:
I. THE HORIZONTAL

THE MOST CASUAL OBSERVER OF the beauties and uglinesses of Nature will have observed that in the anatomy of that very common object, a Tree, there are two widely different classes of branches. The one class grows more or less straight out from the trunk and after a horizontal career droops somewhat at the extremities, the other grows upwards in a persevering and uniform ascent. Such branches when springing high up on the trunk of the tree form the very top of the tree.

But though these facts are patent in vegetable life, and though it is clear that anybody not idiotic and sufficiently active can climb more or less successfully up a tree going higher and higher, and selecting for his ascent the branches that aspire, not making a precarious way along the other class of branch which at the best is horizontal, and at the worst droops downwards, it seems there must be greater difficulties in the ascension of what is known among climbers as the Tree of Society. For while you may see some of them climbing steadily higher, and ever mount-

ing till their electro-plated forms are lost amid
the gold of the topmost foliage, and their joyful
monkey-cries mingle and almost are entuned
with the song of the native birds who naturally
make their nest there, you will see other climbers
—the majority in fact—eagerly scrambling for
ever along perfectly horizontal boughs that
never bring them any higher up at all, and eventually, depressed by their weight, but bend earth-
wards again. Unlike the happier apes who have
a *flair* for altitude and bird-song, these less fortunate sisters have only a *flair* for clinging and
proceeding.

There are of course specimens of these Trees
of Society in every town in England, and specimens of the monkeys who hop about them. But
those are but small trees and the climbers small
apes, and the climbing of these shrubs appears
to present but moderate difficulties. The great
specimen, the one glorious and perfect human
vegetable which grows in England, flourishes
only in the centre of London ; its roots draw
their nutriment from the soil of Middlesex (not
of Surrey), and its top, resonant with birds, soars
high into the ample ether of Mayfair. It is a
regular monkey-puzzle, and swarms with industrious climbers going in every direction, most

THE HORIZONTAL

of them, unfortunately, proceeding with infinite toil along horizontal branches, while others slowly or swiftly make their way upwards. Occasionally, with shrill screams and impotent clutchings at the trunk, one falls, and the higher the fall, the more completely dead will he (or she, particularly she) be when he reaches the ground. She may lie, faintly twitching for a minute or two, while grimacing faces of friends peer down at her, but even before her twitchings have ceased they have turned to their businesses again, for no climber ever has a moment's rest, and a few ghouls crawl out from the bushes and bear away the corpse for interment wrapped up in a winding sheet of the less respectable journals of the day.... Let us study the unnatural history of these curious brightly-coloured creatures a little more in detail.

Dismissing the metaphor of the trees, we may say that at one time or another these climbers have come to London, like Dick Whittington. Possibly they may always have lived in London, taking London as a mere geographical expression, but London, considered as a spiritual (or unspiritual) entity, has at one time or other in their lives dawned upon them as a shining and desirable thing, and they have said to themselves, gazing upwards, 'I want; I want.' They have probably had more than the proverbial half-crown in their pockets, for climbing is an expensive job, with all the provisions and guides and ropes and axes necessary for its accomplishment, and half-a-crown would not go very far. Unlike Dick Whittington, however, they have not brought their cat along with them, but they get their cat, so to speak, when they begin to climb. In other words, without metaphor, they hook on to somebody, a pianist, or a duchess, or a buffoon, or an artist, or a cabinet-minister, or something striking of some kind, and firmly clutch it. Eminence of any sort, whether of birth or of achievement, is naturally a useful aid in ascensions, while on the other hand the climber's half-crowns, or her flattery, or her dinners, or her country-house, perhaps even the climber herself, holds attractions for the particular piece of eminence she has put the hook into. It is her mascot, her latch-key, her passport—what you will—and she is wise to cling on to it for dear life. The mascot may not like it at first, he may wriggle and struggle, but on no account should she let go. Probably he gets accustomed to it quite soon, and does not mind being her electric light which she turns on when she chooses, and,

THE HORIZONTAL

incidentally, pays for quite honestly. The two begin, in a way, to run each other, in most cases without scandal or any cause for scandal, and, mutually sustained, soar upwards together. By means of her mascot she attracts his friends to her house, so that he knows that whenever he goes there he will find congenial spirits and an excellent dinner, while she, if she is clever (and no climbers, whether horizontals or perpendiculars, are without wits), finds herself gently wafted upwards.

She will probably have begun her climb up the first few feet of the branchless trunk with the aid of ladders, friends and acquaintances (chiefly acquaintances) who have introduced her to one or two desirable folk, her mascot among them, and have enabled her to lay her slim prehensile hand on the lowest branches. At this point, having now a firm hold, so it seems to her, she will often kick her ladders down, perhaps not really intending to kick them, but in her spring upwards doing so almost accidentally. But if she does, she commits a great stupidity, and it is almost safe to bet that she will prove a horizontal. For it may easily prove that she will need those same ladders again a little higher up the trunk where there is a hiatus in branches,

149

and returning for them will find them no longer there. They will not be lying prone on the ground as she probably thought (if she gave another thought to them at all), but they will be somewhere the other side of the tree, out of reach. She has to coax them back, and it is possible they will not come for her coaxing. And while she is pondering she may loose hold of her mascot, who will scramble away. In that case, she had better jump down at once, and begin (slightly soiled) all over again.

To take a concrete instance, after this general introduction (as if, after reading a book about some curious and interesting animal we went to the Zoological Gardens to observe its appearance and habits), Mrs. Howard Britten furnishes a good example of the horizontal variety. Where the 'Howard' came from nobody knew or cared; she just took it, and since no one else wanted it, nothing was said. She had married a genial solicitor, who from contact with the dusky secrets of the great, had acquired a liking for their sunlight, and did not in the least object to being put in his wife's knapsack. He made a very large income in his profession, and found that, though household expenses began to mount even quicker than his wife, the house in Brompton Square became considerably more amusing when the climbing began. He took no active part in it, but merely popped his head out of the knapsack and contentedly admired the enlarged view. Nor was he the least surprised when at the end of this particular season, his Molly persuaded him to move Mayfairwards, and purchase (the fact that it was a great bargain made little persuasion necessary) a house in Brook Street with a ball-room.

Molly Howard-Britten (the hyphen appeared this summer) had chosen for her mascot a Member of Parliament who had lately entered the Ark of the Cabinet, and was uncomfortable at home because his wife had an outrageous stammer and an inordinate passion for woolwork. Mr. Harbinger was of course a Conservative, for to the climber that notorious body, the House of Lords, constitutes a considerable proportion of the top of the tree, and the House of Lords is generally supposed to be of the Tory creed. It was safer, therefore, as she looked forward to a good deal of their society, to have a Conservative mascot. She on her side offered a quick feminine wit to amuse him, a charming face and manner, and really admirable food. Mrs. Harbinger came once or twice, bringing

151

her skeins with her, but since she disliked dinner-parties as much as she adored worsted, it soon became common for her husband to dine with the Howard-Brittens alone. The Howard-Brittens spent a week-end with the Harbingers, and there Molly easily secured three or four of his friends to dine with her on the following Friday week. On this occasion one of them was going on to a very sumptuous tree-top ball afterwards, and during dinner she was rung up by the hostess who, agitated by the extreme inclemency of the night, begged her to bring a guest or two more along with her. This was luck: Molly went, and being a remarkably good dancer spent an evening that proved both agreeable and profitable. By the end of the season she had got well placed among the lower branches of the tree, and, perhaps a shade too soon, since it is not quite so easy to be a hostess as might be supposed, took the Brook Street house with the ball-room.

She spent a rather sleepless August with her husband at Marienbad, and began to make her first mistakes. She gave picnics, and being in too great a hurry to secure a crowd, secured the crowd, but unfortunately it was the wrong one. She asked every one to come and see her when

Chinfans : & : The Conjurer.

they got back to England, but those who came were not for the most part the singers in the top branches, but climbers like herself. This fact vaguely dawned on her, and she determined to rectify it when, with the assembling of Parliament in November, her mascot would be in town again. She did rectify it, and in the rectification made things much worse, for she gently dropped all the people she did not want, and made herself a quantity of enemies, not interesting, splendid enemies, whose attention it was an honour to attract, even though that attention wore a hostile aspect, but tiresome, stupid little enemies. Then a stroke of ill-luck, which was not at all her fault, befell her, for in January there was a general election, the Conservatives were turned out, and worse than that, Mr. Harbinger lost his seat. Her attempt to make her house a rallying-spot for the vanquished party signally failed.

Then she made her second mistake. Politics having proved a broken reed, she adopted the dangerous device of pretending to be extremely intimate with her mascot, alluding to him as 'Bertie,' and if the telephone bell rang excusing herself by saying that she must see what Bertie wanted. Had people believed in the intimacy of this relation, one of two things might have

153

happened: she might either have made herself
an object of interest, or (here was the danger),
she might have had a fall. She had not at present climbed very high, so she would not have
hurt herself fatally, but neither of these things
happened. Nobody cared, any more than they
cared about her having added Howard and the
hyphen to her name. Thus an unprofitable
spring passed, and, as a matter of fact, she
was beginning to climb out along a horizontal
branch.

With May there came to town the noted
Austrian pianist, Herr Grossesnoise. His fame
had already preceded him from Vienna, and
remembering that she had once seen him at
Marienbad, Molly Howard-Britten wrote to
him boldly and rather splendidly at the Ritz, re-
minding him of their meeting (he had stepped
on her toe and apologised with a magnificent
hat-wave), and begging him to come and dine
any day next week except Thursday, which she
knew was the evening of his first concert. She
wrote—and here her fatal horizontality came
in—on paper with a coronet and another address on the top, hoping that she might strike
some streak of snobbism. She had come by this
paper quite honestly, having stayed in the house

and having taken a sheet or two of the paper put on the writing-table of her bedroom, obviously for the use of guests. So now she used it, crossing out the address, and substituting for it 25A Brook Street, Park Lane. A favourable answer came, addressed to the Highly Noble Lady Howard-Britten (for he prided himself on his English), on which the Highly Noble scrawled a couple of dozen notes to musical friends and acquaintances (chiefly acquaintances), asking them to dine on the forthcoming fatal Friday, which was the day after Herr Grossesnoise's first recital, to meet the illustrious Austrian.

So far all was prosperous and the climbing weather stood at 'set fair.' It is true that she had changed horses in mid-stream, for in intention she definitely unharnessed poor Mr. Harbinger, and put the unsuspecting pianist in her shafts. But the fatal thing about changing horses in mid-stream is that the coachman usually puts in a worse horse, which Mrs. Howard-Britten had not done, since Mr. Harbinger could not at the present time be considered a horse at all. Already musical London was interested in the advent of her new mascot, for he had been well advertised, and of her twenty-four invita-

tions, nineteen guests instantly accepted, who
with her husband and the Herr would cause
'covers to be laid,' as she was determined the
fashionable papers should say, for twenty-two.
Then she settled to have an evening party
afterwards, and though on the couple of hundred
invitations which she sent out she did not definitely state that Herr Grossesnoise was going
to play, she wrote on the cards 'To meet Herr
Grossesnoise.' But when you see a pianist's
name on an 'At Home, 10.30 R.S.V.P.' it is
not unnatural to suppose that he is going to
be a pianist in very deed. Among these two
hundred she asked a fair sprinkling of people
she wanted to know, but at present didn't, and
had a Steinway Grand precariously hoisted
through the window into her drawing-room and
retuned on arrival. But in these arrangements
her potential horizontality came out more glar-
ingly than ever, for she took a middle course
which no climber ever should. She was inde-
finite, she did not actually know whether Herr
Grossesnoise would play or not. Either she
ought to have engaged him to play at any fee
within reason, if she meant (as she did mean),
to make a real spring upwards to-night, or she
should not have mentioned the fact that he was

coming. As it was, every one supposed he would play, and since his recital the day before had roused a *furore* of enthusiasm in the press, almost all her two hundred evening-party invitations were accepted. A whole section of Brook Street was blocked with motor-cars, and several aspiring Americans who found it impossible to get to their hotel for the present looked in unasked until the road was clear. But as Mrs. Howard-Britten knew no more than a high percentage of her guests by sight, the gratuitous honour thus done her passed undetected.

The evening was a failure of so thorough a description as to be almost pathetic. Herr Grossesnoise played, but not the piano. He came up from the dining-room, slightly rosy with port and altogether inflated with his success, into the drawing-room, set with row upon row of small gilt chairs, and proceeded to do conjuring-tricks in a curious patois of German, French, and English. He insisted on people taking cards from him, and on guessing the cards they had chosen, pressing them continually on his hostess and exclaiming, 'That is the Funf de piques, Lady Howard-Britten.' His colossal form and his iron will permeated the room, while he insisted on doing trick after

157

trick and pointedly addressing his hostess as Lady Howard-Britten, till she got almost to hate the sound of that desired prefix, while all the time the Steinway Grand yawned for him. More bitter than that was the fact that he asked Lady Howard-Britten to play a little slow music ('You play, hein, miladi?') while he did the most difficult of his tricks, and there the poor lady had to sit, when it was he who should be sitting there, and try to remember 'White Wings they never grow whiskers,' or some other waltz of her youth. By degrees the growing fury of her guests generated that force of crowds which no individual can withstand, and in mass they rose and went downstairs, so that by half-past eleven the rooms were empty but for the pianist and his host and hostess. Even then he would not desist, but went on with his ridiculous tricks till she could have cried with fatigue and thwarted ambition.

But no climber sits down over a reverse even as crushing as this, and Mrs. Howard-Britten determined to wipe out her failure with a ball. She got hold of a good cotillion-leader, and gave him practically *carte blanche* as regards the presents, engaged her band, and issued a thousand invitations. When the dancing was at its height there were precisely ten couples on the floor, and every one went home laden like a Christmas tree with expensive spoils.

All that season she was absolutely indefatigable: she tried charity, and engaged a fifty-guinea supper-table at Middlesex House for the evening party on behalf of Lighthouse-keepers. She lent her ball-room for a conference on Roumanian folk-songs given by the idol of the Mayfair drawing-rooms, and standing by the door as the audience arrived shook hands with as many of them as she could. She tried to be original, had a wigwam erected in the same room, and hired a troupe of Red Indians from the White City, who danced and made the most godless noises on outlandish instruments, but somehow the originality of the entertainment was swamped in its extreme tediousness. She tried to be conventional and took a box at the opera, where twice a week she and two or three perfectly unknown young men wondered who everybody was. She hired a yacht for the Cowes week and a depopulated grouse-moor in Sutherlandshire, but for all her exertions she only got a little farther out on the horizontal branch of the tree she so longed to climb. Nothing happened: she made no mark and only spent money, which, after all, any one can do, if he is only fortunate enough to have it.

She labours on, faint and rather older, but pursuing. She is always delighted if any one proposes himself to lunch or dinner, because, with the true climber's instinct, she always thinks it may lead to something. But it is to be feared that all it leads to is that slight drooping of the horizontal bough at the end, and not towards the birds that sing among the topmost branches. She lacked something in her equipment which Nature had not given her, the *flair* for the people who matter, the knowledge of the precise ingredients in the successful birdlime. . . . But her husband never regrets the Brook Street house with the ball-room. He plays Badminton in it by electric light on his return from his office.

CLIMBERS:
II. THE PERPENDICULAR
CHAPTER NINE

CHAPTER NINE
CLIMBERS :
II. THE PERPENDICULAR

IF YOU ARE AN OBSERVANT PERSON addicted to washing your hands and face, you can hardly fail to have noticed the legend 'Whitehand' imprinted on your basin and soap-dish, and, indeed on every sort of crockery. Probably, if you thought about it at all, you imagined that this was a trade-name, alluding to the effect of washing, but it is not really so at all. Mr. Whitehand is the kind American gentleman who supplies so many of us with these articles of toilet, and as a consequence Mr. Whitehand is rich if not beyond the feverish dreams of avarice, at any rate, as rich as avarice can possibly desire to be in its waking moments.

This fortunate gentleman began life as a boy who swept out a public lavatory in New York, and this accounts for his turning his attention to hardware. When he had made this colossal fortune he set about spending it, though he had no chance of spending it as quickly as it came in, and with a view to this bought a large chocolate-coloured house in Fifth Avenue, a cottage at Newport, an immense steam-yacht, a complete train in which to go on his journeys, and ordered a

163

few dozen of Raphael's pictures and some Gobelin tapestry. He was never quite certain whether Gobelin had painted the pictures and the firm of Raphael the tapestry, but that did not matter, since he had them both. He then expected his wife to get him into the very best New York society, and enter the charmed circle of the Four Hundred. She had been his typewriter, and in a fit of moral weakness, of which he had never repented, since she suited him extremely well, he had married her. But whether it was that the Four Hundred had seen too much of Mr. Whitehand's name on their slop-basins, or whether he had not bought sufficient Raphaels, they one and all turned their ivory shoulders on him and his wife, and banged the door in their faces. As Mrs. Whitehand had just as keen a desire to shine among the stars of the amazing city as her husband, she was naturally much annoyed at her inability to climb into the firmament, the more so because she was convinced that with practice she could become a first-rate climber. She had the indomitable will and the absolute imperviousness to rebuffs that are the birthright of that agile race, and felt the inward sense of her royalty in this respect, as might some Princess over whom a wizard had cast a spell. But some-

how, here in New York, she got no practice
in climbing, because she could make no beginning whatever. She could only stand on tiptoe,
which is a very different matter. And when at
the end of her second year of standing on tiptoe,
Nittie Vandercrump, the acknowledged queen
of Newport, cut her dead for the seventeenth
time, and with her famous scream asked her
friend, Nancy Costersnatch, who all those
strange faces belonged to, Mrs. Whitehand
began to think that New York was impregnable
by direct assault. But in the manner of Benjamin
Disraeli, she vowed that some day she would
attract attention in that assembly, and with Nittie Vandercrump's scream ringing in her ears,
sat down to think.

Well, there were other places in the world
besides New York, places where there grew
social trees of far greater antiquity and magnificence, and she settled to climb the London tree.
But she felt that she would get on better there
at first without her husband. He was rather
too fond of telling people what he paid for his
Raphaels and how fast his special train went.
When she had climbed right up among the topmost branches, she would send for him, and let
a rope down to him, and he might quote as many

prices as he chose, but she felt with the unerring instinct of a born climber that he would be in the way at first, even as he had been in New York. She talked it over quite amicably with him that night, while the still air vibrated with the sound of the band next door and the screams of Nittie, and he cordially consented to the experiment. Money *ad libitum* was to be hers, and it was to be her business to get somewhere where the screams of Nittie would be no more to them than the cries of the milkman in the street. He, meantime, was to amuse himself with the special train and the Gobelin tapestry and the steam-yacht, and make himself as comfortable as he could, while his wife made this broad outflank-ing movement on New York.

So one May afternoon Sarah Whitehand, with twenty-two trunks and a couple of maids and her own indomitable will, arrived at the Ritz Hotel in Piccadilly, and set about her business. She dined alone in the restaurant, read the small paragraphs in the evening paper, and ordered a box at the opera. She was an insignificant little personage in the way of physical advantages, being short, and having a face which owned no particular features. She had, it is true, two eyes, a nose and a mouth, for the absence of any of

166

them would have made her conspicuous, which she was not, but there was nothing to be said about them. They were just there: two of them greenish, one of them slightly turned up, while the other was but a hole in her face. She was not ugly any more than she was pretty; she was merely nothing at all; you did not look twice at her. But if you had, it might have struck you that there was something uncommonly shrewd about the insignificant objects which supplied the place of features. Also, when she was determined to do anything, you would have seen that she had a chin.

But to-night this face of common objects rose out of the most wonderful gown in shades of orange that was ever seen. It was crowned too in a winking splendour of diamonds that shouted and sang in her sandy-coloured hair, and round her neck were half-a-dozen rows of marvellous pearls. While the curtain was up she sat close to the front of her box with her eyes undeviatingly fixed on the stage, and when the curtain fell she stood there a minute more, so that the whole house should get a good view of her. She did not look about her; she merely stood there, seemingly unconscious of the opera-glasses that were turned on her from all quarters of the

167

house. All round, everybody was asking everybody else who the woman with the diamond Crystal Palace was, and nobody knew. Nor did anybody know, not even Mrs. Isaacs, the fashionable clairvoyante, who exposed a considerable portion of her ample form in the stalls, that through the mists of the horizon there faintly shone to-night the star of surpassing magnitude that was to climb to the very zenith, and burn there in unwinking splendour.

For the next week Sarah took no direct step forward, but sat in the Ritz Hotel, or in her box at the opera, or drove about on shopping errands. Among these latter must be included a quantity of visits to house-agents, who had in their hands the letting of furnished houses in such localities as Grosvenor Square and Brook Street, and what seemed to interest her more than the houses themselves was the question of who was wishing to let them. But she was in no hurry: she was perfectly well aware that the first steps were of the utmost importance, and before she stepped at all, she wanted to find the largest and strongest stepping-stone available. The evening usually found her alone in her opera-box, seemingly absorbed in the presentation of Russian ballet, and unconscious of

Chambers: The Perpendicular

the opera-glasses levelled at her. She gave the opera-glasses something to look at too, for she never appeared twice in the same gown, but in a series of last cries, most stimulating to the observer. One night she wore a sort of bonnet of ospreys on her head, and again everybody asked everybody else who the Cherokee Indian was. But again nobody knew, and so they all supposed that the ospreys were made of celluloid. But they had an uncomfortable idea that they might be genuine. But if so, who's were they? London began to be genuinely intrigued.

After about a week of this, she suddenly lighted upon exactly what she had been looking for in the books of the house-agents. A certain new big house in Grosvenor Street, which externally recalled a fortress made of stout sandbags was to be let by Lord Newgate (marquis of), the eldest son of the Duke of Bailey. Sarah had already seen Lady Newgate, a tall, floating dream of blue eyes, golden hair and child-like mouth, at the opera, and knew her and her husband to be among the true white nightingales who sing and play poker at the very top of the tree she was pining to climb. A less Napoleonic climber than she might have thought that to take the Newgates' house was a passport to

169

CLIMBERS

London, but she knew that it would only carry its cachet among the people who could not really be of any use to her, namely, that well-dressed esurient gang of Londoners who find it quite sufficient to be fed and amused at other people's expense. Sensible woman that she was, she fully intended to feed and amuse them, but it was not they that she was out for: at the best they were like the stage army which marches in at one door and out at another, and in and out again. They were not the principals. You were, of course, surrounded by people whom you fed and a-mused, if you were on the climb, just as you were surrounded by footmen and motor-cars, but she looked much further than this. She argued, again correctly, that if such conspicuously mel-odious songsters as the Newgates wanted to let their house during the very months when they would naturally be needing it most, they must be in considerable want of money, and would be likely to give some valuable equivalent for it. So, seeing her scheme complete from end to end, as far as the taking of this house was con-cerned, she told the slightly astonished agent that she was willing to take the house for the next three months or the next six at the price named, but that she wished to make her arrangements with Lady Newgate herself. The agent, seeing that she was just a wild American, politely represented to her that this was not the usual method of doing such business in civilized places, but she remained adamant.

'If I don't settle it up with the Marchioness of Newgate,' she said, 'I won't settle it up with anybody else. Kindly give that message over your 'phone, please, to the Marchioness, and say that if she feels disposed to entertain my proposals, I shall be very happy to see her at the Ritz Hotel this afternoon. And if she don't care to come, why, I don't care to take her old house. That's all. You may say that my name is Mrs. Whitehand, and that my husband's the head of the firm, which she maybe has heard of.'

Now simple as this procedure appeared, it had the simplicity of genius about it, not the simplicity of the fool. As far as houses went, she did not care whether she had Lady Newgate's house or a house in Newgate. What she was going for was Lady Newgate. It was possible, of course, that on receiving this message, Lady Newgate would simply say, 'What on earth does she want to see me for? She can settle it through the agent.' If that was the case, it was not likely that Lady Newgate would be any good

171

to her. But it was quite possible that Lady Newgate might say, 'Hullo: here is *the* Mrs. Whitehand going about looking for a house, and probably unchaperoned.' Anyhow there was a
chance of this, and since Sarah Whitehand had
nothing to lose, she took it. For there might be
something to gain, and these are the best chances
to take.

Now the price asked for this fortress of marble
and cedar-wood was an extremely high one, and
the Newgates would have been perfectly willing
to take about half of the sum named, after a little
genteel and lofty bargaining. Consequently the
prospect of immediately obtaining the full price,
not for three months only, but for six, including
August and September, when an aged caretaker
usually had it for nothing, was irresistibly attractive. Toby Newgate, it is true, momentarily
demurred against his wife's waiting upon the
peremptory Yankee at the Ritz, but she had seen
much further than him with her forget-me-not
coloured eyes. She had seen in fact just as far
as Mrs. Whitehand.

'My dear, it's flying in the face of Providence
to neglect such a chance,' she said, 'and if she'd
told me to wait at the bottle entrance of the Ele-
phant and Castle I should have gone.'

THE PERPENDICULAR

He shuffled about the room a little.

'Don't like your being whistled to by the wife of the manufacturer of hardware, just for six months' rent,' he said.

She laughed.

'My dear Toby, it isn't only six months' rent that's at stake,' she said. 'I'm not going to be landlady only, I expect, but godmother.'

'Godmother?'

'Yes, dear, and you godfather to Mr. Hardware, if he is here. But you needn't buy any presents. Good American godchildren give the presents themselves.'

Toby had some vague sense of her position, she only the necessity of his poverty.

'You mean you're going to trot them round?' he asked.

'Yes, if possible. I think her message means that. Why else should she want to see me, or take the house for August and September? It's a bribe, a hint, a signal.'

The interview between the two ladies was extremely satisfactory, as is usually the case when there is no nonsense about the conversationalists, and each of them is willing and even eager to give exactly what the other wants. The business of the house was very soon relegated to a firm

of solicitors, and the godmotherly aspect began
to show through the form of the landlady, as in
some cunning transformation scene, faintly at
first but with increasing distinctness.

'Your first visit to London?' asked Madge
Newgate.

'Yes: I've been here but a week, and have
done nothing but hunt around for a house and
go to the opera.'

Instantly Lady Newgate remembered the
solitary and dazzling figure in the box. She, too,
had wondered who the woman in orange and diamonds was. Mrs. Whitehand's face had made
no impression whatever on her.

'Ah, then I am sure I saw you there,' she said.
'We were all wondering who you were. You
must allow me to put some of my friends out of
their suspense by letting them know.'

Mrs. Whitehead laughed.

'I should be very pleased for your friends not
to strain themselves,' she remarked. 'And I'm
in suspense too, as to who your friends are. I
don't know a soul in London.'

This was rather a relief to Madge Newgate.
Sometimes a perfectly impossible tail was attached to these strange Americans, and you had
to encounter the riff-raff of the Western world

en masse. She laid her hand on the other's knee.

' My dear, you must get some friends at once,' she said. ' You might dine with us to-night, will you? I have two or three people coming.'

This was quite sufficient. Mrs. Whitehand spoke shortly and to the point.

'I want to be run,' she said.

Madge Newgate was a perfectly honest woman, and now that all ambiguity had been cleared away, she explained what she could do and what she would expect to receive. She could give Mrs. Whitehand the opportunity of meeting practically any one she wished, and she could repeat and again repeat that opportunity. She could bring people to Mrs. Whitehand's house, and within limits get them to invite her to theirs. But more than that, she frankly admitted she could not do.

' I can't make them your friends,' she said. 'I can only make them your acquaintances. The other depends on you. You must show yourself useful or charming or striking in some way, if you want more than just to go to balls and dinner-parties. Luckily in London we are very hungry, so that you can always feed people, and very poor, so that you can always tip people, and very dull, so that you can always amuse people.'

175

CLIMBERS

'I see: I quite see that,' said Mrs. Whitehand.

Madge felt that she understood: that it was worth while explaining.

'I'm sure you will forgive my plain speaking,' she said, 'but it is never any use being vague. And there's a lot of luck about it. Sometimes a very stupid woman "arrives" and a very clever agreeable one doesn't, and the Lord knows why. I should be quite American do you know, if I were you; Americans are taking well just now. About—well, why should I beat about the bush? —about what I am to receive for my trouble. I imagine you don't want my house in the least for the three months after July, and I am willing to take a good deal of trouble for your renting it then. And when some more rent is due, I think I had better tell you, hadn't I? I am not greedy, I am only very poor.'

Now no climber could possibly have made a better beginning than this. Sarah Whitehand could not have chosen a more admirable god-mother, and though she was lucky in having hit on precisely the right one, she had shown true perpendicularity in having gone to the right class. She had aimed at the best and hit it, and in the three months that followed she continued to show a discretion that bore out the early pro-

mise of her talents. She neither gave herself airs,
nor was she grovellingly humble, she merely
enjoyed herself enormously, and since of all
social gifts that is the most popular, she rapidly
mounted. She threw herself, with Lady Newgate's sanction, into artistic circles, and firmly
annexed as her mascot the chief dancer of the
Russian ballet. Unlike poor horizontal Mrs.
Howard-Britten, with her disappointing Herr
Grossesnoise, she made it quite clear that when
she asked a party to meet a bevy of Russian
dancers that party was surely going to see the
bevy dance, which it did quite delightfully under
the stimulus of enormous fees. She did not
waste her quails and champagne on unremun-
erative guests, or guests who so far from helping
her would only hinder her, but followed Lady
Newgate's directions precisely as to whom she
should ask, and very good directions they were.

She had other modes of access as well. She
flattered grossly or delicately as the occasion
demanded. When she saw that some one liked
to be drenched in flattery she had bucketsful
of it ready. At other times she confined herself
to telling So-and-so's friends how lovely So-and-
so was looking, or how brilliant So-and-so was.
This method she chiefly adopted to those of

CLIMBERS

Lady Newgate's friends who had somewhat unwillingly come to her house, and plentiful applications of these gratifying assurances usually had their effect sooner or later, for Sarah Whitehand knew that nobody is insensible to flattery, if (and here lay the virtue) the proper brand properly administered was supplied. Sometimes the case required study : it was no use conveying to a beautiful woman the flattery of acknowledging her beauty : you had to find out something on which she secretly prided herself, her tact or her want of tact, her charming manners or her absence of manners, her toes or her teeth, and make little hypodermic injections in the right place. Then again there were people who in spite of all allurements would have nothing to do with her. After two or three unsuccessful direct assaults, she would attempt that no more, but, just as she was outflanking New York by laying siege to London, outflank those obdurate folk by laying siege to their friends. She was infinitely patient over these operations, and nibbled her way round them, until they were cut off, and found themselves devoid of all friends save such as were friends of the accomplished Sarah. By patience, by good humour and by her own enjoyment she

THE PERPENDICULAR

moved steadily and rapidly upwards on branches
that she gilded beforehand. She often thought
about Nittie Vandercrump screaming away in
New York, and even adopted a modified version
of her yells of pleasure. These she gave vent to
when dull people, who for some reason mattered,
told her long stupid stories, and found that they
had achieved, for the first time in their lives, a
brilliant and startling success.

Naturally she made quantities of mistakes.
Occasionally a man at her table would find in
his neighbour a woman with whom he had not
been on speaking terms for years, or again, she
solemnly introduced Bob Crawley to the wife
he had divorced a year before, and immediately
afterwards to the woman concerning whom his
wife might have divorced him the year before
that. Nor could she at first grasp the fact that
a Duchess perhaps did not matter at all, and
that Mrs. Smith mattered very much, and she
had to drop the Duchess and smooth down Mrs.
Smith. But these were mere childish stumbles,
and having picked herself up she again clung
tightly with one hand to her godmother and
with the other to her mascot, the Russian
dancer.

And all the time while she was so nimbly

climbing, she and Petropopoloffski were sitting
on a great egg which was to be hatched in the
autumn, when London would be full again for
the session. Russian ballet this year was the
rage to the exclusion of all other rages, and
the great egg was no less than a further six-
weeks season of it, financed and engineered by
Sarah. Not until when late in July the egg was,
so to speak, announced, did any one, even her
godmother, know that it was she who had laid
it, and she who had Petropopoloffski in her
pocket, and she who had taken the Duke of
Kent's theatre for it, and she who had arranged
to have the dress-circle and pit taken away and
rows of boxes substituted, and she, finally, who
had taken thirty-seven boxes herself, so that
only through her favour could anybody engage
them. It was a great, a brilliant stroke, hazard-
ous perhaps, but then everybody wanted to see
Russian ballet so much that they would not
stick at being indebted to her for their boxes.
But it came off: within a couple of days of the
subscription list being opened, all boxes not
reserved by her had been let, and she began
most cordially to allow applicants to have some
of hers. Very wisely, she gratified no private
spites by refusing them, she only made friends

by granting them. She kept just two or three of the best, in case of emergencies.

And so she goes on from height to height. Mr. Whitehand was duly sent for in the succeeding spring, and sat entranced for a month, as in a dream of content, in this Valhalla of the gods. But he found he could not stand much of the rarefied air at a time, and so bought a large place in the country, where in leather gaiters he feels like an English squire, and has revolutionized all the sanitary arrangements of the house. And when Nittie came to London, as she did during the summer, and screamed a welcome to her darling Sally, her darling Sally was very wise about it, and instead of kicking her down, which she might easily have done, she gave her a leg-up by asking her to a particularly dazzling dinner-party and being quite kind to her. She does not see much of her, but always treats her with the respect and pity due to a poor relation. There is no more climbing to be done here, and for a change next autumn she means to go downstairs to New York and see how they are all getting on in the kitchen.

THE SPIRITUAL
PASTOR
CHAPTER TEN

CHAPTER TEN
THE SPIRITUAL
PASTOR

ST. SEBASTIAN'S CHURCH, SITU-
ated in the centre of Mayfair, is justly famous
for the beauty of its structure, the excellence of
its singing, the splendour of its vestments and
the magnificence of its vicar, Mr. Sandow, who
might well be taken, as far as superb physical
proportions go, to be the show-pupil of his
hardly less illustrious namesake. He is 'Hon.'
and 'Rev.,' but he prefers his letters to be addressed to him as 'The Rev. the Hon. J. S.
Sandow' instead of 'The Hon. the Rev.,' for,
as he says, the 'Hon.' is an accident—not, of
course, implying that there was any irregularity about his birth—and that 'the Rev.' is
the more purposeful of his prefixes. To do him
justice, he lives up to this fine pronouncement,
and while, if his brother, Lord Shetland, lunches
with him he is regaled with the simplest of family
meals, he entertains an athletic Bishop who is
a friend of his with the sumptuousness due from
a Rev. to a Prince of the Church, and takes him
down in a motor to Queen's Club, where they
have a delightful game of racquets together.

185

THE FREAKS OF MAYFAIR

His ecclesiastical politics, as exhibited in the services at St. Sebastian's, are distinctly High. But they are also Broad, since for those of his parishioners who prefer it, there is an early celebration at 8 A.M. conducted by two of his curates. Matins, sung in plain-song by an admirable choir, follows at 10 A.M., and this is usually attended by a packed congregation. By eleven, in any case, which is the hour for the sermon, there is not a seat to be had in the church, for Mr. Sandow invariably preaches himself, and from Pimlico and the wilds of South Kensington, from Bayswater and Regent's Park, eager listeners flock to hear him. This is no quarter of an hour's oration: he seldom preaches less than fifty minutes, and often the large Louis Seize clock below the organ loft, with its discreetly nude bronze figures of Apollo and Daphne in the vale of Tempe sprawling over it, chimes noon on its musical bells before he has finished. A short pause succeeds the conclusion of the sermon, and the choir enters the church again from the vestry in magnificent procession and panoply of banners, followed by the clergy in full vestments. Clouds of the most expensive incense befog the chancel, and if what is enacted there is not the Mass, it is an uncommonly good imitation of it.

Mr. Sandow's ecclesiastical doctrines thus preach themselves, so to speak, in the manner of this service, and there is little directly doctrinal in his sermons. He ranges the religions of the world, culling flowers from Buddhism, Mohammedanism, Fire Worship, Christian Science, and has even been known to find something totemistic, if not positively sacramental, in the practice of cannibalism. The first part of these sermons is always extremely erudite, and out of his erudition there springs a sort of sunlit Pantheism. He splits no hairs over it, and does not insist on any definitely limited meaning being attached to the word 'immanent'; it satisfies him to prove the pervasiveness of Deity. At other times, instead of rearing his creed as this substructure of world-religion, he mines into the sciences and gives his congregation delightful glimpses into the elements of astronomy, with amazing figures as to the distance of the fixed stars. Or he investigates botany, and Aquilegia rolls off his tongue as sonorously as Aldebaran. Out of the arts as well, from music, painting, sculpture he delves his gold, that gold which he finds so freely distributed throughout the entire universe. Having got it, he becomes

187

the goldsmith, and shows his listeners how to turn their lives into wondrous images of pure gold, the gold of the complete consciousness that there is nothing in this world common or unclean, or less than Divine. He snaps his fingers in the face of Satan, and tells him, as if he was a mere Mrs. Harris, that there is no 'sich a person.' All is divine, and therefore we must set about our businesses with joy and exultation. Not only will sorrow and sighing flee away, but they actually have fled away: it is impossible that they should have a place in the world such as he has already proved the existence of by the aid of botany or music or cannibalism. Indeed if it were possible to conceive the existence of sin, we should, we could only expect to find it where, by reason of people not realizing the splendour of those realities, they allow themselves to be depressed or gloomy. And (since the Louis Seize clock has already chimed) Now.

There is no doubt that this robust joyousness suits his congregation very well, for most of the inhabitants of his parish, the owners of nice houses in Curzon Street and Park Lane and other comfortably-situated homes, have really a great deal to be jolly about, and Mr. Sandow points out their causes for thankfulness in patches so purple that they almost explode with richness of colour. Another great theme of his, when for a Sunday or two he has made his hearers feel how lucky all mankind is to be born into this glorious world, is the duty of kindliness and simplicity. Indeed his collected sermons rather resemble the collected works of Ouida, who could write so charmingly about pairs of little wooden shoes, and with the same pen, make us swoon with the splendours of Russian princesses, and the gorgeousness of young guardsmen with their plumes of sunny hair, and their parties at the Star and Garter hotel where they throw the half-guinea peaches at the fireflies.* If joy is the violins in this perfect orchestra of a world, simplicity and kindliness are, according to Mr. Sandow, the horns and the trombones. Crowned heads are of no account to him if accompanied by cold hearts, but he has found (greatly to their credit) that the inhabitants of splendid houses, and the owners of broad acres are among the simplest and kindliest of mankind, and he often takes an opportunity to tell them so, ex cathedra, from his pulpit. And since it is impossible not to be gratified in hearing a pro-

* A fact.

189

fessional testimonial, publicly delivered, to your merits, his unbounded popularity with his congregation is amply accounted for, and the offertories at St. Sebastian's rain on him, as on some great male Danae, showers of gold.

At the convenient hour of six, so that devotional exercises should not interfere with tea or dinner, Vespers are celebrated with extreme magnificence. The church blazes with lights, which shine out through clouds of incense, and the air is sonorous with the splendour and shout of plain-song. And at eleven (evening dress optional) is sung Compline. Here Mr. Sandow makes a wise concession to the more Anglican section of his flock, and the psalms are sung to rich chants by Stainer and Havergal and the Rev. P. Henley, while the hymn is some popular favourite out of the Ancient and Modern book. Though evening dress is optional, and no beggar in rags, should such ever present himself, would be turned away, evening dress is the more general, for many people drop in on their way home from dinner, and the street is a perfect queue of motor-cars, as if a smart evening-party was going on. And then you shall see rows of brilliant dames in gorgeous gowns and tiaras, singing lustily, and young men and maidens and

THE SPIRITUAL PASTOR

solid substantial fathers all in a row, with their fat chins rising and falling as they rumble away at Rev. P. Henley in their throats. For certainly Mr. Sandow has succeeded in making religion, or at any rate attendance at Sunday services, fashionable in his parish: it is the Thing to go to church, though whether like other fashions, such as diabolo or jig-saw puzzles, it is a temporary enthusiasm remains to be seen.

On week-days the devotional needs of his congregation are not so sumptuously attended to, for Mr. Sandow, certainly as wise as most children of light, is aware that his flock are very busy people, and does not care to risk the institution of a failure. Besides he has very strong notions of the duty of every man and woman to do their work in the world, even if, apparently, their work chiefly consists in the passionate pursuit of pleasure. But he likes splendour (as well as simplicity) in those advantageously situated, just as he likes splendour in his Sunday services. He is, too, himself, a very busy man, for since he makes it his duty to know his flock individually, and since his flock are that sort of sheep which gives luncheon and dinner-parties and balls in great profusion, it follows that he has a great many invitations to these festivities, and accepts

191

THE FREAKS OF MAYFAIR

as many as he can possibly manage. But he always practises the observance of fasts, and never eats meat on Fridays. To make meagre on Fridays and vigils therefore has become rather fashionable also, and since most of his entertainers have excellent chefs, Friday, though a meatless day, is an extremely well-fed one, for with salmon trout and caviare, and a dish of asparagus and some truffles, and an ice pudding and some soufflé of cheese, you can make a very decent pretence of lunching, especially if particularly good wines flow fast as a compensation for this ecclesiastical abstinence. It is a pastime for hostesses also to exercise the ingenuity of their chefs in producing dishes, strictly vegetarian, in which a subtle combination of herbs and condiments produces a meaty flavour, and to observe Mr. Sandow's face when he thinks he tastes veal. But he is formally assured that no four-legged or two-legged animal has as much as walked into the stew-pot, and in consequence, with many compliments, he asks for a second helping.

All this endears Mr. Sandow to his people; they say, 'He is so very human and not the least like a clergyman.' He would not be pleased with this expression if it came to his ears, though

THE SPIRITUAL PASTOR

if he was told he was not in the least like most other clergymen there would be no complaint. For he thinks that the office of a priest is to enter into the joys and pleasures of those he ministers to, not only to exact their attendance at church, and, as he modestly says of himself, 'bore them stiff' with his interminable sermons, and who shall say he is wrong? Indeed to see him at a ball, it is more the other guests that enter into his pleasures than he into theirs, for he is one of the best dancers that ever stepped, and there is a queue of ladies, as at the booking-office of Victoria Station on a Bank Holiday, waiting to have a turn with the Terpsichorean vicar. But, like some modified Cinderella, he keeps early hours, and vanishes on the stroke of one, in order to be up in good time in the morning, and at his work. For in addition to all his parties, his interviews, his dances, his Sunday services, his games of racquets, he has a further life of his own, being a voluminous and widely-read author.

This literary profession of his is no mere matter of a parish-magazine, or of letters to the *Guardian* about the Eastward position, or the *Spectator* about early buttercups, but he publishes on his own account at least two volumes

193

every year. Usually those take the form of essays, written in the second or pair-of-wooden-shoes manner, and probably each of them contains a greater number of true and edifying reflections than have ever before appeared between the covers of a single volume. It is no disparagement of them to say that they seem to go on for ever, for so do the waters of a spring, except in times of such severe drought as is unknown to the pen of this ready writer. They all begin in an enticing manner, for Mr. Sandow tells you how he was walking across the Park one morning, when he observed two sparrows quarrelling over a piece of bread that some kind bystander had thrown them. This naturally gives rise to reflections as to the distressing manner in which ill-temper spoils our day. The kind bystander is, of course, Providence, who throws quantities of bread, and Mr. Sandow tells us that it is the truer wisdom not to behave like silly sparrows and all wrangle over one piece, but hop cheerfully away, with a blessing, in the certainty of finding plenty more. Or again Mr. Sandow describes how he was hurrying to the station to catch a train, fussing himself with the thought that he would not be in time for it, and not noticing the limpid blue of the sky and

194

the white clouds that floated across it. When he came to the station he found he had still five minutes to spare and so need not have hurried at all, but drunk in the gladness of God's spring. From this lesson, he humbly hopes, he will be less disposed to fuss in the future, but trust to the wise hand that guides him. We are not told what would have been the moral if Mr. Sandow had missed his train, but then, after all he did not write about that, and one can only conjecture that it would have been a lesson to him as to how to wait patiently (picking up edifying crumbs at the station) for the next train. Or he sees a house in process of being pulled down, with gaping wall showing the internal decoration, and tenderly wonders what sweet private converse took place in front of the denuded fire-place. His vivid imagination pictures charming scenes: on one wall on the third story was a paper with repeated images of Jack and Jill and Red Riding Hood and Little Miss Muffit, and he conjectures that here was the nursery, and the paper looked down on children at play. But the children are grown up now; they have outlived their nursery, as we all do, but instead of regretting days that are no more we must go on from strength to strength, till we reach the imperish-

195

able house of many mansions which nobody will ever pull down. At the end of each of these musings written in the pair-of-wooden-shoes mode comes a passage of this kind in the second manner, a sudden purple patch about imperishable houses, or the towers of Beulah, or the dawning of the everlasting day.

It is just possible that this skeleton-analysis of Mr. Sandow's works may faintly produce the impression that there is something a shade commonplace about them, that they lack the clarion of romance, of excitement, of distinction in thought, or whatever it is that we look for when we read books. And it is idle to deny that this impression is ill-founded: no flash of blinding revelation ever surprises the reader, nor does he ever feel that the perusal of them has added a new element to or presented a fresh aspect of life; only that here, gracefully expressed, is precisely what he had always thought. This probably is the secret of their amazing popularity, for there is nothing more pleasing than to find oneself in complete harmony with one's author. Anybody might have written them, provided only he had a fluent pen and an edifying mind. Mr. Sandow never gave one of his readers, even the most squeamish and sensitive, the smallest

THE SPIRITUAL PASTOR

sense of discomfort or anxiety. He flows pleasantly along, faintly stimulating, and though he suggests no soul-questionings that could possibly keep anybody awake o' nights, a very large number of the public are delighted to read a little more in the morning. For Mr. Sandow never fails you; his fund of mild and pleasant reflection is absolutely unending, and if from a mental point of view the study of his works is rather like eating jam from a spoon, you can at least be certain that you will never bite on a stone and jar your teeth. And if you do not by way of intellectual provender like eating jam, why, you need not read Mr. Sandow's books, but those of somebody else.

7

'SING FOR YOUR DINNER'
CHAPTER ELEVEN

CHAPTER ELEVEN
'SING FOR YOUR DINNER'

THAT AMIABLE LITTLE FOWL, the Piping Bullfinch, has very pretty manners. If he is a well-bred bird, as most Piping Bullfinches are (though they come from Germany), he will, when he sees you approach his cage, put his head on one side, make two or three polite little bows, and whistle to you with very melodious and tuneful flutings. But it is not entirely his love of melody that inspires him, for he is rather greedy also (though he comes from Germany), and perhaps the politeness of his bows and the tunes that he so pleasantly pipes, would be considerably curtailed if he found that he was not generally given, as a reward for his courtesy, something equally pleasant to eat. But if he feels that you are willing to supply him with the morsels in which his rather limited soul delights, he will continue to bow and pipe to you until he is stuffed. And, as soon as ever his appetite begins to assert itself again (and he is a remarkably steady feeder), he will resume his bows and his tunes.

Quite a large class of people, the numerical

majority of which consists of youngish men, may be most aptly described as Singers for their Dinner or Piping Bullfinches. Girls and young women are not of so numerous a company, for if unmarried they have generally some sort of home where they are given their dinners, without singing for them, or if married are occupied in their duties as providers to their husbands. But there is a large quantity of young or youngish unmarried men who, living in bachelor chambers or flats, find it both more economical and pleasanter to sing for their dinner than to eat it less sociably at their own expense at their clubs or to entertain others, and they are therefore prepared to make themselves extremely agreeable for the price of their food. The bargain is not really very one-sided ; indeed, as bargains go it is a very tolerably fair one; for there are great handfuls of people who, either from a natural dislike of old friends or for lack of them, are constantly delighted to see a Piping Bullfinch or two at their tables. They even go further than this, and take these neat little birds to the theatre or the opera (paying of course for their tickets), and invite them down to weekends in the country and to shooting-parties. Thus their houses are gay with pleasant conversation, and the Piping Bullfinches have better balances at their banks.

Leonard Bashton is among the most amiable and successful of these birds. He lives in two pleasant little rooms in a discreet and quiet house that lies between Mount Street and Oxford Street, for which he pays an extremely moderate rent. Exteriorly the street has little to recommend it, for it is narrow and shabby, and at the back, Number 5, where his rooms are situated on the first floor, looks out on to mews. These, a few years ago, would not have been agreeable neighbours just outside a bedroom window, but Leonard had the sense to see that with the incoming of motors there would be fewer horses, so that before long the disadvantage of having mews so close to the head of his bed would be sensibly diminished. Thus, being a young man of very acute instincts, he procured a yearly lease of these apartments, with option on his side to renew, at a very small rental. In this he has reaped a perfectly honest reward for his foresightedness, since horses nowadays are practically extinct animals in these mews, and similar sets of rooms on each side of him are let for twice the sum that he pays for his.

He has no profession whatever except that

of a piping bullfinch, for on attaining the age
of twenty-one he came into a property of £400
a year, and for the next three years lived with
his widowed mother in a country town, declin-
ing politely but quite firmly (and he is not without considerable force of character on a small
scale), to take up any profession whatever. He
was in every respect (except that of not working for his living), an excellent son to Mrs.
Bashton, but when his two elder brothers, one
a soldier, the other in the Foreign Office, came
to stop with her, he always made a point of retiring to sea-side lodgings for the period of their
stay, since he objected to their attitude towards
him. But on their departure, he always came
swiftly back again, and continued to be a charming inmate of Mrs. Bashton's house, entertaining her rather dull friends for her with excellent
good humour, playing bridge at the county club
between tea and dinner, and if the weather was
fine and warm, indulging in a round of golf,
usually on the ladies' links, in the afternoon.
But all this time he was aware that he was in
the chrysalis stage, so to speak, and with a view
to becoming a butterfly before very long, made
a habit (his only indulgence) of reading a large
quantity of those periodicals known as Society

papers, which chronicle the movements and marriages of the great world. Without knowing any of these stars by sight, except when he had the opportunity of seeing their pictures in the papers, he thus amassed a great quantity of information about their more trivial doings, and advanced his education. In the same way his assiduity for an hour or two every day at the bridge-tables in the club, enabled him to play a very decent game. He never lost his temper at cards (or indeed at anything else), nor wrangled with his partner, nor did he lose his head and make impossible declarations. These qualities in this feverish, ill-tempered world caused him to be in general request when a card-party was in prospect, and also kept him in pocket-money. He did not win much, but he averaged, as his note-book of winnings and losings told him, a steady pound a week. And as he did not spend much, for he had no expensive tastes of any sort or kind, he found his cigarettes and his disbursements at the golf-club were paid for by his gentle winnings. Subsequently, on his mother's death, he came into a further £200 a year, and after careful calculation felt himself able, since now board and lodgings were no longer supplied him gratis, to move to London, and by whistling his tunes, and making his bows, manage to procure for himself a really nice little cage with gilded wires, and plenty of food.

He soon anchored himself in the 'ampler ether' of town. He did not take any steps to cultivate his brother in the Foreign Office or his brother's friends, but at once began to establish a position with such friends of his mother who had town-houses. He was not in any hurry to do this, and after he had been asked to tea twice, but never to any more substantial entertainment by one of these, he refused his third similar invitation, since perpetually going to tea was not a sufficiently substantial reward for his bowings and pipings. On the fourth occasion he was asked to lunch, and being put next a most disagreeable cousin of his hostess's who had come up to town for the day in order to alter her will, he made himself so perfectly charming to her that his hostess, in a spasm of gratitude, asked him to go to the opera with her the week after. This he very kindly consented to do, and having good eyes and an excellent memory was able to point out to her from the box several of the mighty ones of the earth, whose portraits he had seen in picture-papers. He did not exactly say he knew any of them, but went so far as hinting as much. 'There is old Lady Birmingham,' he said, remembering what he had read that morning. 'Look, she has the big tiara on. She gave a huge party last night with a cotillion. I suppose you were there, weren't you? No; I couldn't go. Such a lot on, isn't there, just now?'

His hostess, Mrs. Theobald, one of those industrious climbers who are for ever mounting the stairs which, like the treadmill, bring them no higher at all, was rather impressed by this. It was also gratifying to find that Leonard supposed that she had been to Lady Birmingham's party, which she would have given one if not both of her fine eyes to have been invited to. Of course she said that she hadn't been able to go either, which was perfectly true, since she hadn't been asked, and enquired who the woman with the amazing emeralds was. There again Leonard was lucky, for in the same paper he had read that Mrs. Cyrus M. Plush had been at Lady Birmingham's party, wearing her prodigious emeralds, five rows of them and a girdle. It was exceedingly unlikely that anybody else had five rows and a girdle, as this new-comer into the box opposite certainly had, and he replied with great glibness:

207

THE FREAKS OF MAYFAIR

'Oh, Mrs. Cyrus Plush. Just look at her emeralds. How convenient if you were drinking *crème de menthe* and spilt it. People would only think that it was another emerald. I don't think she's really very good-looking, do you?'

Everybody has probably experienced the horror of getting one drop of honey or some other viscous fluid on to the inside of his cuff. Though there is only just one drop of it, its presence spreads until the whole arm seems to be sticky with it. In such quiet mysterious sort Leonard began to spread. Mrs. Theobald, the desire of whose life was to entertain largely, asked him regularly and constantly to her dinner-parties, and her guests extended their invitations to him. He took this set of rooms, of which mention has been made, and with considerable foresight did them up in the violent colours which were only just beginning to come into fashion. It was no part of his plan to indulge his new friends with expensive entertainments, but just now, strawberries being so cheap, he found it an excellent investment to ask two or three ladies to tea, and found that four invitations to tea usually brought him in three invitations to dinner, which was a good dividend. To employ a smart tailor was another necessary out-

lay, and he affected socks of the same colour as
his brilliant tie, and carried a malacca cane with
a top of cloudy amber. But soon, always quick
to perceive the things that really interested him,
he saw that though he was getting on quite
nicely with women, their husbands and brothers
did not seem to think much of him, and he abandoned the malacca cane, and took up golf again.
Before long he hit a very happy kind of mean,
and made himself the sort of young man who is
not out of place either in town or in the country.
He had several invitations to country-houses
during the months of August and September,
and when he came back to settle in London again
in October, he got elected to a club of decent
standing, and may be considered launched. His
keel no longer grated, so to speak, on the sand:
he was afloat in a shallow sea of acquaintances,
with no sort or kind of friend among them.

Leonard was in no way a snob, and did not,
having been launched, want to voyage the deep
seas. He had not the smallest regard for a Marchioness as such, and his regard was entirely
limited to those who would make him comfortable. Naturally, if a Marchioness asked him to
tea, he went, but he did not go on drinking tea
with a Marchioness if that was to be the limit

of her hospitalities. All his respect for money, similarly, was founded on the basis of what other people's money would procure for him, and while he would take a great deal of trouble to secure a footing in a comfortable house, he would not raise a little finger to be put in a poky attic in the mansion of a millionaire. But he remained assiduous in reading paragraphs about those who move in the world which is called smart, because he knew that other people liked to hear about it, and he continued to give the impression that he himself frequented exalted circles. But since he was not himself employed in climbing, he did not drop his early friends, so long as they put plenty of nice things through the bars of his cage.

He has no intention at present of marrying, since even to marry a rich wife would interfere with his career, and he is certainly incapable of falling in love with a poor one. Indeed he neither falls in love nor pretends to with anybody, not being of the type that desires amorous, or even philandering adventure. The motto of his life is 'Comfort,' and on his £600 a year, he finds that warm houses, good cooks, the use of motor-cars, all the things in fact which supply the wadding of life and take away its sharp cold angles are

well within his reach. He is an excellent hand-
ler of money, has no debts at all, and last season
even managed to have a stall at the opera two
nights a week. This again proved an excellent
investment, for he often gave it away in remun-
erative quarters, and when he occupied it himself, spent all the time between the acts in visiting
the boxes of his friends, and pointing them out
any celebrity who might happen to be present.
Nowadays he knows them all by sight, and so
has less cause to read the Society journals. The
time that he used to give to that he now spends
more healthily in walking swiftly for an hour
every morning round the Serpentine, for he is
beginning to exhibit slight signs of stoutness.
But he hopes with this increase of exercise to
keep at bay the threatened increase of weight.
When he meets another piping bullfinch, he is
dexterous in his cordiality, and by urging him in-
definitely to come to his 'diggings,' often secures
a definite invitation.

Leonard has now been a full-fledged piping
bullfinch for eight years and has arrived at the
age of thirty-four. Since he is not in the least
ashamed of his whole life, there is probably no
one in the world who has less to be ashamed of.
Neither the ten commandments, nor the grand

text in Galatians which entails twenty-nine distinct damnations can catch him tripping. He is uniformly good-natured, he has never set himself to make his way by telling scandalous stories about other people, he pays his debts, he is perfectly honest, almost abstemiously sober, and the more closely you cross-examine him, the more spotlessly free from any sort of vice does he seem to be. Only, if you stand a little way off, so to speak, and take a general view of him, he is somehow horrible to look upon, for it would seem that he has no soul of any kind, either good or bad. And that, when all is said and done, is a grave defect: there is nothing there, and it is just that which is the matter with him. All those delicious dinners feed a non-existent thing; all those nice clothes clothe it; all his amiable conversation reveals it.

His future is depressing to contemplate, for already he is a man governed no longer by impulse or reason, but by habit. Habit has become the dominating influence in his life, and at the age when all men ought to be learning and possibly preaching, he is only practising his terrible little doctrine of the piping bullfinch. If he could fall in love even with a barmaid that would be the best that could happen to his immortal soul, or if, obeying impulse, he could only develop a craving for drink or indeed a craving for anything, there would still be some sign of vitality in the withered kernel of that nut of his spiritual self which was never cracked. It is always better to go to the good than to go to the bad, but quite frankly it is better to go to the bad than to go nowhere at all. But, as it is, it seems as if only the frost and the fat were going to congeal more closely round his atrophied heart. He is a prey to that worst craving known to mankind, the craving for being comfortable. Any disreputable adventure might save him, for it might teach him that there are such things as desire and longing for no matter what. Surely to desire fire is better than merely to expect a hot-water bottle in your bed.

But it is to be feared that even at this early age of thirty-four he is a hopeless case. His engagement book is filled to repletion, and he lunches and dines every day with pleasant acquaintances, and during the slack months of London stays with them in their pleasant houses. He makes 'rounds' of visits; all August and September, all January and all April he is in the country, quartered on people whom he does not care about, and who do not care about him.

THE FREAKS OF MAYFAIR

But he is always so pleasant; he always knows everybody, and when the men come out of the dining-room in the evening he always sinks into a chair beside a rather unattractive female, and converses quite amusingly to her till he is summoned to the bridge table. Then he always says he is being 'torn away,' and promises to tell her the rest of it to-morrow morning. And the bereaved lady thinks what a nice man Mr. Bashton is. And so he is.

But as years go on he will get a little lazier and a little stouter. Gradually he will be relegated to the second line, and the young piping bullfinches who succeed him will in the chirpiness of their early songs wonder why that 'old buffer' still assumes the airs of youth. He will still appear in the smoking-room with the stories that were once of contemporaneous happenings, and now seem to the young birds tales of ancient history. By degrees his country visits will dwindle, for country-houses are so draughty, and he will sit and snooze in his club, presenting the back of an odious bald head to the passer-by in St. James's Street, as he waits for the familiar crowd to return to London again after the Christmas holidays. His contemporaries will have tall sons and daughters growing up

round them, and he will be familiarly known as
Uncle Leonard, and yet all the time he will
think he is something of a gay young spark yet,
and point out Lady Birmingham's daughter
and Mrs. Cyrus Plush's son to his neighbour at
the opera.

Then some day, if fate is kind, he will have
a fit and die without more ado. Not a single
person in the world will really miss him, for the
very simple reason that there was nobody really
there. He will have touched no heart, he will
have nothing and have produced nothing but
the little songs and bows that younger bullfinches perform with so much more verve. Somebody at the club when he no longer takes a
sheaf of newspapers under his arm will say,
'Poor old Bashton: nice old chap! Getting
awfully doddery, wasn't he? Are you going to
see the new play to-night? Haymarket, isn't
it?'

THE PRAISERS OF
PAST TIME
CHAPTER TWELVE

CHAPTER TWELVE
THE PRAISERS OF
PAST TIME

EVER SINCE SOCIETY (WITH A large S) has been the subject of Gleanings and Memoirs and Memories and Recollections, the distinguished authors of these chatty little volumes have been practically unanimous in saying that in their day things were very different, and such goings-on would not ever have been allowed then. (They would express it in a statelier manner, but that is the meaning they seek to convey.) Incidentally, then, if we may take it that these strictures accurately represent facts, we may gather that most of those writers must be listened to with the deference due to the elderly (since otherwise they would not be able to remember such a very different state of things), and that they are none of them much pleased with the way in which People (with a big P) behave now. This appears to be a constant phenomenon, for if we delve into social history of any epoch we find just the same complaints about the contemporary world, and we are forced to conclude that, to state the case broadly, uncles and aunts and grandfathers and grandmothers never approve of the behaviour of their nephews, nieces, and grandchildren. At least those who write about them do not, as they take the gloomiest view of them, and are unanimous in declaring that the country is going or has gone to the dogs.

Now there is a great deal of indulgence to be granted to these loquacious pessimists, who are full of a faded sort of spice and are seldom dull. Indeed, they should be more indulgent to themselves, and oftener remember that it is but reasonable that they should have lost the elasticity of youth, and the powers of enjoyment that no doubt were once theirs, the failure of which leads them to contrast so sadly (and peevishly) the days that are with the days that are no more. But they in their time caused a great deal of head-shaking and uplifting of horror-stricken hands on the part of their elders, and, remembering how little notice they ever took of those antique mutterings, they would be kinder to themselves and to others if they put their ink-bottles away, and looked on at the abandoned revellers who take no great notice of them as comfortably as possible, instead of sitting up to all hours of the night composing liverish reflections about the wickedness of the young men

220

and women of the day. It is a waste of good
vitriol to throw it about like that, and it is really
wiser to wipe the hot ink from the pen before
and not after writing, as one of our most industrious social castigators did not so long ago,
'There is not an ounce of manliness in the
country.' For contradiction of so Bedlamitish
a sentiment the myriad graves in France and
Flanders bear a testimony that is the more elo-
quent for its being unspoken.

The truth is that every age finds a great deal
to condemn in the manners and customs that
differentiate the rising generation from its own.
But that does not prove that the elders are right:
if it proves anything it proves that they are too
old to take in new ideas, and so had better con-
fine their remarks to the old ones, on which they
are possibly competent to speak. For in their
view, if we take the collective wisdom of the
moralists of Mayfair, the country is not now for
the first time going to the dogs, but has always
been going to the dogs. It has never done anything else, and yet it has not quite arrived at the
dogs yet. But the cats appear to have got it.

There has always been, since man became a
gregarious animal, a vague affair called Society.
Nobody knows precisely what it is except that

THE FREAKS OF MAYFAIR

when the gregariousness of man attained sufficient dimensions it happened, and the older
generation disapproved of it. The more elderly
specimens of cave-men without a shadow of
doubt deplored the manner in which the younger
gnawed their mutton-bones, and regretted the
days when all well-regulated cave-boys and
cave-girls always wiped their greasy fingers not
on their new woad as they now do, but on their
hair. Society used to be society then, and only
the well-mannered could get into it. And it is
in precisely the same tone that the modern moralists croon or croak their laments beside the
waters of the modern Babylon. The present
praisers of past time bewail with an acidity that
betokens suppressed gout that their nephews
and nieces have lost all decency in speech, and
actually make public the fact that one or other
of them has had appendicitis. And Uncle cannot bear it! Have appendicitis if you must, but
for the sake of Society pretend that it was a sore
throat unusually low down. At all costs Uncle's
Victorian sensibilities must be spared, or he
will go straight home and embark on Chapter
IX. of his Recollections, called the 'Moral De-
pravity of Modern Society.' But is it too late
for him to remember how once the Queen of

THE PRAISERS OF PAST TIME

Spain caught fire, and was badly burned because nobody could allude to the awful fact that she had l–gs? The elderly ladies-in-waiting would have died rather than have done so, and therefore the Royal L–gs were much injured by the flame. But perhaps Uncle would like that.... Or again our truculent admonishers remind us that Society was once a very small and esoteric body. Nobody but the de Veres really counted, just as if the de Veres prehistorically came down from heaven with the Ark of Society in their possession and thereupon started it. But nobody really started it; the de Veres did not as a matter of fact say, 'Let there be Society,' and there was Society. Once the de Veres themselves were parvenus: when they began to enter the charmed circle they too were accounted nobodies, and the ante-de Veres wondered who Those People were. It was but gradually that the mists of antiquity clothed their august forms, until, as from the cloud on Sinai, they looked down on the post-de Veres, and mumbled together at the degeneration of that which had once been *so* select and is now so Verabund.

The great central Aunt Sally at which the memorio-maniacs hurl their darts most viciously is a thing they call Smart Society, or the Smart

THE FREAKS OF MAYFAIR

Set. For generations they have done so, and the poor Aunt Sally ought to have been battered to bits long ago, for they throw their missiles straight at her face from point-blank range. Only, by some process not rightly understood by her assailants, she appears perfectly impervious to their attack and proceeds on her godless way as brightly as ever. She is also, as we shall see, largely an invention of those who so strenuously denounce her. What started the loquacious pessimist perhaps was that he found there were a good many nephews and nieces who enjoyed themselves very tolerably, and began to find him and his tedious stories about what the best people did in the age of Henry II. or Charles I. or William IV. (according to the epoch which he remembers best) rather tiresome, and did not listen to him with due attention. That may or may not have set him going, but the fact that there exists in London a quantity of rich people who like to entertain their friends (among whom the loquacious pessimist would scorn to number himself) fills him with ungovernable fury, and with a pen that blisters the paper, he describes how they spend their Sunday.

Breakfast, if we may believe him, goes on

from ten till twelve, lunch (a substantial dinner) is prolonged with liqueurs and cigars till close on tea-time, when sandwiches and even 'bleeding woodcocks' are provided. Dinner is not till nine, and so late an hour finds everybody hungry again. Then, forgetting that he has told us that eating goes on the whole day, he informs us in another attack on poor Aunt Sally that these same people spend Sunday in riding and driving and going out to tea ten miles away, and careering about on a 'troop' of bicycles. Yet again, forgetting that here his text is the sinful extravagance of the present day, he informs us how stately were the good old times, when a rich man kept as many servants as he could afford and 'sailed along' in a coach and four, instead of going (as he does in these shambling, undignified days) in the twopenny tube. . . . After all, the economy effected by using the twopenny tube instead of the coach and four would enable you to buy an occasional 'bleeding woodcock' for your friends, and yet not be so extravagant as your good, stately, simple old grandfather. Or, when they speak of modern shooting-parties these chroniclers allude to the mounds of 'crushed pheasants' that are subsequently sent to be sold at the poulterer's, and speak of the hand-reared

225

birds that almost perch on the barrels of their murderers. It would be interesting to place one of these moralists at a modern pheasant-shoot, when the birds rocket above the tree-tops, and see how large a mound of crushed pheasants he mowed down, and how many hand-reared birds came and sat on his gun before he slaughtered them. Such descriptions as these are rank nonsense, the work of outsiders who, while betraying a desolate ignorance of what they are talking about, betray also, in ignorance, an unamiable desire to scold somebody.

Now every one has his own notion of what Society (with a big S) is, and most people mean different things. Guileless snobs read the small paragraphs in the paper, and think they are learning about it. Others walk in the Park and are sure they see it: the suburbs think that it is the sort of circle in which their pet actor habitually moves: South Kensington thinks it is in Park Lane, or the private view of the Academy, or at a garden-party. In point of fact it is, if anywhere, everywhere, and the only thing that can certainly be stated about it is that those who think about it at all, think that it is just a little way ahead, and thus declare themselves to be snobs or ineffectual climbers. But those who

THE PRAISERS OF PAST TIME

really make Society are not those who think about it, but Are it, just because they live the life in which their birth and their circumstances have placed them, with simplicity of mind and enjoyment. Society does not live in a spasm of social efforts, it lives perfectly naturally and without self-consciousness. It is impossible to make anything of your environment if you are always wishing to be somewhere else, and you will make nothing of any environment at all, unless you are at ease there. Indeed the big S of Society is really the invention of the snobbish folk who are not friends with their surroundings, and that in part, at any rate, is why the loquacious pessimist is so unrelenting towards it.

Society, then, and in especial Smart Society, as it exists in the minds of the praisers of past time and of snobs, is a perennial phantom, which is the chief reason why none of them can be forced or can succeed in getting into it. As they conceive of it, it is no more than a Will o' the Wisp, which, if they pursue it, merely leads them on through miry ways to find themselves in the end pursuing nothing at all, and hopelessly bogged in the marshes of their own imagination. That society exists all the world over is, luckily, perfectly true, but this peculiar and

THE FREAKS OF MAYFAIR

odious conception of it is the invention of those who want to get into it and of those who fulminate against it. Indeed it is almost allowable to wonder whether these two classes are not really one, for it is impossible to acquit some of its bitterest enemies of a certain hint of envy in their outpourings, a grain of curiosity in their commination services.

The pity of it is that they will not rest from these strivings, or realize that what they pursue (either with longings or vituperation) exists only in their own excited brains. Each has his feverish dream: one pictures a heavenly Salem of dukes and duchesses, another a swimming bath full of champagne and paved with ortolans, another an Elysium where infinite bridge consumes the night, and continual changing of your dress the day. These conditions have no existence; they are Wills o' the Wisp. There does not exist in the world a Smarter Set (to retain the beloved old snobbism) than a circle of friends who, with definite aims of their own, and tastes that are not copied from other people, enjoy themselves and are at ease with each other, not being snobs on the one hand or grousers on the other. All other ideas of Smart Sets, whether in London or Manchester or

THE PRAISERS OF PAST TIME

the Fiji Islands, are mere moonshine : the only Smart Set that ever existed or ever will exist is that of uncensorious and simple people who have the sense to appreciate the blessings they so richly enjoy. Of these Smart Sets there are many, but they are not the Smart Sets or the capital-lettered Society that are usually meant when allusion is made to them.

But somehow the notion of the existence of 'A Smart Set' or Society with a big S is so deep-rooted that it will be well to examine the evidence for its existence before labelling it 'Bad Meat,' to be destroyed by the Board of Moral Health. The evidence in favour of its existence (if they insist on it) is derivable from three possible sources :

(i.) First-hand evidence of those who have witnessed or partaken in these ungodly orgies.

(ii.) Report.

(iii.) Reporters.

Now the purveyors of the intelligence, those who distribute it, are largely the praisers of past time, who so persistently attack it and paint such lurid pictures of its Neronism. But they must have got their information from some-where (unless we are reluctantly compelled to suppose they made it up) and they can have

THE FREAKS OF MAYFAIR

got it from no other sources than those speci-
fied above.

But on their own fervent asseverations they
have never so much as set foot in these Med-
menham Abbeys, and if their information is derived directly from the Abbeys, it must have
been conveyed either by the revellers themselves, by their valets and ladies' maids, or have
grown out of the Tranby Croft trial. It is unlikely that the revellers should have recounted
the story of their shame to those sleuth-hounds
on the trail of decadence, and if we rule out the
Tranby Croft trial as not covering all that the
sleuth-hounds say about Smart Life, we must
conclude that they must have induced (no doubt
with suitable remuneration) the gentleman's
gentleman and the lady's lady to say what their
owners did and when they went to bed. But not
for a moment can we believe that these distinguished scribes resorted to such a trick. The
statement of the proposition shows how incredible it is, for these high-minded moralists simply
could not have applied for the knowledge of 'sich
goings on' from chattering servants.

First-hand evidence, then, being ruled out,
the purveyors may have derived their information from report. Here the baffled aspirants to

230

the social distinction of being Smart may have helped them. But still such knowledge if worth anything must be based on something, and if on report it is merely the more valueless for having gone through so many mouths.

We are left then with the question of evidence derived from reporters, and here I think we touch the source of the appalling state of things pictured by the loquacious pessimist. The delightful anonymous author of the Londoner's Log-book has grouped the organs of those who chronicle social happenings under the title of Classy Cuttings, and it is from these columns that we must conclude that the praisers of past time derive their awful information. It is they who give to the thirsty public the details of the menu of the supper that followed the dance, and hint how great were the losings of a certain Countess who lives not a hundred miles from B-lgr-v- Sq-r-, when she played poker at St-l-n-. But, does that sort of information carry the required conviction? Indeed it only carries conviction of the lamb-like credulity of the person who believes it. Once upon a time an eminent and excellent lady revealed to a horrified audience that the Smart Set habitually drank what she called 'White Cup' at tea (sensation). It sounded thoroughly Neronian, but lost its impressiveness when the further revelation was made that at a tennis-party certain individuals had been so lost to all sense of decency as to partake of hock and soda instead of tea and cream.

It is on such foundations, columned by Classy Cuttings, that the praisers of past time build the Old Bailey, where, bewigged and berobed, they so solemnly pronounce the extreme sentence on Smart Sets and Society. We must not deny to their summing-up something of the gorgeously Oriental vocabulary of Ouida, though we cannot allow them much share in her wit. She told in the guise of fiction the sort of thing which the praisers of past time—after consulting Classy Cuttings—expect us to accept as facts; she and Classy Cuttings mixed the effervescent beverage which they allow to get flat, and then label it the beef-tea of Fact. And when we are offered these fantastic imaginings and are assured that the lurid pictures are positively photographic in their accuracy, all our pleasure, as readers, is gone, and we expire with a few hollow yawns. We had hoped it was Ouida, but to our unspeakable dismay we are told that it is all Too True. Not being able to swallow that, we can but re-

232

THE PRAISERS OF PAST TIME

member the story of Dr. Johnson and the hot potato.

Tempora mutantur, and unless we change with them we shall never grasp the true values of the marching years. Society (with a final curse on the large S) changes, and the changes represent on the whole the opinion of people who are on the right lines. The praisers of past time have cried 'Wolf' too often with regard to the decadence they invariably detect in the present time, and until we are more certain that at last the wolf is really there, it is wiser to push along than to trust in the denunciations of those who, firmly immured in the sedan-chairs of sixty years ago, squint through the chinks of their lowered blinds (lowered, lest they behold vanity) at the crowd they do not know, and the bustle that they altogether fail to understand. In their day they kicked up their heels much higher than their grandmammas approved. They disregarded the denunciations of their elders then, and they must not be surprised if the younger generation, whose antics their creaking joints and croaking minds are unable to imitate, think of them as antique and peevish progenitors now. The arts of fifty years ago are doubtless theirs, all except the art of gracefully retiring. Instead, the more accomplished of them, since their loquacity no longer can hold an audience, proceed to volumes of uncomprehending memoirs. As long as they stick to the past, their recollections often possess an old-world fragrance as of lavender-bags shut in disused Victorian wardrobes, but when they come to the present the lavender-scent fades, and they reek of brimstone and burning. A grandmamma, talking of past days, is a delightful and adorable member of any circle, but when she laments the dangerous speed at which trains go nowadays, every one younger than she feels she does not quite understand. And if, getting her information from fiction (as the praisers of past days do from the columns of Classy Cuttings), she tells us that motors habitually run over a hundred thousand people a day in the streets of London, the younger folk, with the kindness characteristic of youth, merely shout in her ear-trumpet, 'Yes, Grandma, isn't it awful?' and wonder when her maid will fetch her to go to bed.

It is on Grandma's data that the praisers of past time form their notions of society. She prides herself on never having been in one of those horrible automobiles : the praisers pride themselves on never having set foot within the doors of these unspeakable temples. Apparently

234

THE PRAISERS OF PAST TIME

it is for this reason that they can tell us with pre-
cision what happens there, except when they
forget what they have previously written, and
flatly contradict themselves. Like the Fat Boy,
the loquacious pessimist wants to make our flesh
creep, and sepulchrally announces that he saw
Miss Wardle and Mr. Tupman 'a-kissing and
a-hugging.' But unlike the Fat Boy, who really
saw it, the pessimist has only 'heard tell of it'
in Classy Cuttings, and with Wardle we should
exclaim, 'Pooh, he must have been dreaming.'
So he was, all alone one night when nobody had
asked him out to dinner, and falling into a reverie
proceeded to contrast the Sancta Simplicitas of
the days when everybody sailed along in a coach
and four with those extravagant times when he
has to pay for his own mutton-chop, and rich
folk save their money to go in the twopenny
tube. This sounded a little illogical, but it would
do, and refreshing himself with another drink
of Classy Cuttings, he lashed out at the poker-
party at St-l-n-, by way of punishing those who
were not his hosts on that terrible occasion. Of
course he would not have gone in any case, since
he has never and will never set foot in those
restaurants (not homes) of vice and extravagance. One cannot help wondering whether,

if he condescended to go there, he would not feel a little kinder after ortolans and a bleeding woodcock for tea, and with greater indulgence to the degeneration he deplores, write a few pages about Progress instead of Decadence. But who knows? The ortolans might disagree with him, and he would become unkinder than ever. Possibly all is for the best.